To El
with your

KIDNAPPED IN
JERUSALEM

regards

by
Beatrice Fairbanks Cayzer

Beatrice Cayzer

ISBN: 978-1-64314-144-2 (Paperback)

AuthorsPress
California, USA
www.authorspress.com

Contents

DEDICATION

By disregarding painful teachings,
they found a gentle God.

I dedicate this book to Dr. Philip
Rylands in recognition of his immense
contribution to Florida's Culture since his
arrival in Palm Beach.

List of CHARACTERS

Deedee's story

1930 Palm Beach, Florida

Chapter 1

Deedee Murray, age three
Hon. Ambassador "Jack" Murray, her father
Fraulein von Hubmeyer, her Nanny
Dennis McLeary, Eighteen-year old chauffeur
Ian Blunt, Dennis McLeary's employer
Nellie Combe, fourteen-year-old girl seducer
Mrs. Combe, Nellie's mother, Mr. Blunt's cook

Chapter 6

Two girls in Bathing Suit store, one
from Kusadasi
Two Saudi thugs
U.S. Vice Consul
Passport forger

Chapter 7

Tel Aviv, Israel, Bombay and Digboi,
India, 1948
Aime'e female seducer
Frances Patel, expert on camels
Owner, bad-tempered employer selling
champion camel DESTINY to a Saudi
prince

Chapter 8

Customs shed Riyadh, Saudi Arabia
and Racing Camels' Jockey rooms

His Royal Highness, a son of the King
Suspicious Customs Officer
Andy. Camels' groom

Chapter 9

Camel Races near Riyadh
Youssef, ex-camel jockey a Bedouin
who guards dilapidated house
in desert
Youssef's nameless daughter

Chapter 10

Kuwait oil camp, the capital: Kuwait
City, and Oman with Strait of
Hormuz
Oil-man Alf, rescuer and hopeful
seducer
Beryl, a Quaker offering a welcome
trolley of food and offers her passport

Herb, an American Muslim, of dubious faith

Uncle, Herb's exceedingly wealthy Kuwaiti uncle who has a mysterious black box

Air pirates

Two pilots who fly Uncle's private airplane.

RMS DEVERON's medical officer

Sally, a Quaker convert who gives the address of her Meeting

Chapter 11

London, England mid-September 1948

Claridge's doorman

Wheeler's Restaurant's Maitre D

Coutts Bank Manager and assistant

Euston Road Meeting House's four expectant mothers

Mosque Iman

List of Chapters

Also by Beatrice Fairbanks Cayzer*
TALES OF PALM BEACH (as
Beatrice de Holguin)
THE PRINCES AND
PRINCESSES OF WALES
ROYAL ECCENTRICS (with
Barbara Cartland)
ROYAL LOVERS (with Barbara
Cartland)
THE ROYAL WORLD OF
ANIMALS
DIANE (PRINCESSE DE
POLIGNAC)
MURDER BY MEDICINE
THE HAPPY HARROW
MURDER TRILOGY
MURDER TO MUSIC
MURDERED MOTHERS
MURDER IN MARRIAGE
VAMPIRE MURDERS
LOVE LOVE IN DARFUR
THE HARROW QUARTET
MURDER FOR MUNITIONS

MODELS MURDERED IN MILAN

MOCKING MURDERS IN MADRID

MEXICO'S MOVIELAND MURDERS

MURDER FOR BEAUTY

THE SECRET DIARY OF MRS. JOHN QUINCY ADAMS

TO SAVE A CHILD

KENNEDYS IN LOVE

NEW TALES OF PALM BEACH

Beatrice Fairbanks Cayzer comes from an illustrious family. Her two ancestors who came to Upper Virginia on the Mayflower in 1620 helped found their community. Her mother's uncle was US Vice President Charles Warren Fairbanks. Her father was a US Ambassador at large who negotiated the Peace Treaty of the Peruvian Ecuadorian war. She graduated from Barnard College, and shortly after wed the grandson of a President of Colombia, Alfred Holguin. Her second husband was British cavalry officer Major H. Stanley Cayzer, grandson of Sir Charles Cayzer who founded five shipping companies that eventually had 123 ships under one flag. His uncle Admiral Lord Jellicoe served as First Sea Lord, and later

Governor General of New Zealand. Major Cayzer was a Director of the family firm British & Commonwealth, that has become Caledonia Investments. As a sportsman Stanley Cayzer won the Wokingham race at Royal Ascot and took the Stewards' Cup at Goodwood. He owned with Beatrice the 14,000 acres Cabrach estate in Aberdeenshire and Westcote Manor in Warwickshire, he was MFH of the Warwickshire Hunt. Beatrice founded the Cayzer Museum for Children, and then turned to a LITERARY CAREER. In Oxfordshire she wrote THE PRINCES AND PRINCESSES OF WALES. In Guernsey she wrote THE ROYAL WORLD OF ANIMALS. Returning to the USA she wrote eleven novels about British racehorse trainer Rick Harrow, winning the Book Of The Year Award from the International Horseracing Writers Society. In 1988 she authored DIANE, a biography of Princess de Polignac.

In 2016 she married environmentalist William Richards II, and settled in Palm Beach.

She had a sell out with THE SECRET DIARY OF MRS JOHN. QUINCY ADAMS, in 2017 she had very favorable reviews for TO SAVE A CHILD, and in 2018 had another sell out with NEW TALES OF PALM BEACH. In 2019 her KENNEDYS IN LOVE was turned into a film..

Deedee's story

Chapter 1

January 1930 Palm Beach, Florida

I was three years old, drowning.

Fraulein Hubmeyer, nanny to my sister Elaine and me, had insisted on braving the unexpectedly high rollers on the in-fashion North End Beach.

That day she had played chauffeur to Daddy and me. Fraulein, an Austrian from Vienna, was an avid swimmer and had hired herself to be a governess when she learned that my family wintered in Florida.

Daddy, legally blind in both of his soft brown eyes, could see enough to read and handle himself thanks to thick lenses that protruded from heavy black frames that grooved his nose.

By noon Fraulein had braved crashing waves until she lost her footing, was swept past the safety of a sand bar, and we were drowning.

"SECOURS, SECOURS," she screamed in French, forgetting in which country she was drowning.

Daddy heard the shouts. Tossing his eyeglasses to the wet sand, he stumbled toward the tide line where he realized quickly that he could not swim well enough to save us. Turning away from the tumbling waves, Daddy climbed through the resisting sand to the line of cars that studded North Ocean Boulevard at the top of the beach, crying out to the lounging drivers: "Save my child. Save her nanny."

From between a Model-T Ford and a tired Rolls Royce, a teenager Dennis McLeary emerged. He was outfitted in a borrowed uniform that was far too large: the chauffeur cap with its emblazoned RR sliding on his ears, and the knickerbockers threatening to expose his briefs for want of a belt.

He aimed straight for Daddy, pulling off cap, jacket, and knickerbockers to arrive in only his briefs to reach Daddy's side. His employer, Ian Blunt, a stockbroker long settled in Florida, pointed a cigar like a sword at him, while scolding: "Where do you think you are going, Dennis-Smith McCleary? Get back in the Rolls, at once!"

No other chauffeur answered Daddy's desperate cries; nor had any of the beach goers. All were staring at the drowning scene as if it was part of a new Hollywood film.

Dennis McLeary—eighteen at that time—stopped a few seconds next to Daddy, shouting: "Wut ye pay? Sayin' I saves 'em, Wut Ye Gonna Pay? Ten, uh, ten thousand?"

Daddy's head, like a jack-in-the-box, nodded agreement.

"Write it down. Ten thousand to Dennis-Smith McCleary," the boy tossed back, racing toward the menacing surf.

I knew none of that. I'd lost consciousness. But, I was at the edge of regaining enough to know I was dying, when I felt a huge tug on the criss-cross straps of my swimsuit.

Air! I opened my mouth for it and swallowed more water.

Soon I'd been perched around the boy's neck, while he pulled along Fraulein by her chin in the crook of his right arm.

He rode the incoming waves with the skill of a born-to-it surfer. This boy knew the ocean. I heard the crunch of his feet hitting sand, lost consciousness again, and came-to hearing Fraulein weeping with joy.

Now she used her native language. "Gott ist gut. Gott ist gut. Gott ist gut," She kept repeating, like a mantra, or as if she'd gone demented.

A busybody pushed aside my hovering Daddy: "I've been a girl scout. I know what to do for people who nearly drowned."

First, she worked on me, giving me CPR then turned me on my right side, stretched out my arm and bent a leg to the knee.

I vomited.

Gently, she massaged my chest to expel the seawater. I vomited again.

She pressed her mouth to mine and gave me mouth to mouth resuscitation.

I sat up. Daddy squeezed me, with tears polka-dotting his weird eyeglasses.

The busybody turned to Fraulein to further practice her expertise. But there was no mouth to mouth. She straddled Fraulein and rhythmically worked her fingers as if Fraulein's rib cage was a keyboard.

Fraulein resisted this inept lifesaving technique. After waving away the busybody, she didn't sit up until some time later and when she did, she reached out toward Daddy's free arm, and begged pardon for taking me into the ocean. Now she had tears too. Was she afraid of losing her job?

She didn't. Daddy consoled her, patting her blue shoulder. He muttered: "I know you've had a terrible experience. And you could've saved yourself by letting go of Deedee."

Only then did Daddy turn from me and Fraulein . He assured the muscular boy who'd saved us: "Your money will be transferred from my New York bank to keep my promise."

Dennis McCleary, already correctly in his dry chauffeur's outfit, had been leaning from one muscular leg to the other toward Daddy, with what was almost a threatening stance.

His name was in the local newspaper: not for saving Fraulein and me from drowning, but for "engaging in sex with a girl under the age for a 'consenting adult' plea." The suggested sentence? Twenty years without parole.

Chapter 2

New York City, 1947 Columbia University and Cathedral of St. John the Divine

During the next seventeen years, I shuttled to schools of various denominations. To get my Bachelor's Degree, I went to Barnard College. From there, I continued on at Columbia University to try to earn a Masters in Social Studies.

One of my obligations was to join a Social Studies group that had access to rooms where aspiring students could work with troubled people. I chose the room nearest to where deep armchairs, free tea and cookies were provided.

My Social Worker room was designated to help ex-convicts accustom themselves to the reality of a free citizen's life. The first case of an ex-jailbird I was allotted turned out to be that of Dennis Mcleary, who'd saved my life from the waves pounding off the Northernmost of Palm Beach's playground beaches.

Neither of us could have known what the other had grown to look like. I was a post-deb who had my father's bad eyesight and wore thick lenses although they weren't as weird as Daddy's. My frenzy for chic clothes had evaporated after that deb year. In 1947, I favored knee-length skirts and loose sweaters albeit that Christian Dior had launched the lower-calf look with fitted jackets.

At the age of three I'd been a blonde, although with my hair so wet from the near-drowning Dennis could not have known that.

By 1947, I was a brunette, with thick chestnut color hair.

I barely recalled the muscular teenager of that 1930 day, although the carrot-red shade of his hair was so intense it had been noticeable even though wet.

Still very much a red-head, with eyebrows to match, Dennis didn't have the expected blue eyes. Instead, his eyes were an intense green.

He was tall, now, six feet two, but not muscular. Instead, he looked emaciated. His eyes were deep in their sockets, his arms spindly. A very short jailbird haircut indicated that he'd been in prison very recently. Without any introduction, when he caught me looking at his haircut, he muttered: "Short hair protects against lice."

Dennis didn't take a seat in my cramped unadorned office. He peered at me strangely, while adopting a mixed stance. What was his age? Thirty-five?

I felt he was like a sinking ship in a storm approaching a lighthouse.

Did he expect me to be his lighthouse?

"Your name, Deedee Murray? I read it on the list of Social Workers. Same as Jack Murray's? The Ambassador wut sent me my money?"

I'd sent the ten thousand dollars, plus the interest earned in his savings account, to Dennis McCleary after he was released from prison. Three years had been erased from his twenty years sentence "for good behavior."

He'd alerted our Murray family lawyer that he'd opened a bank account in New York City. He'd moved from Palm Beach County, due to being listed there as a sex offender. Daddy and Mummy were both dead by then, and I'd taken over the responsibility of keeping Daddy's promise.

When I'd seen his name on the list of unfortunates scheduled for my Social

Work duties, I knew there would be no surprises for me because I'd followed the name Dennis McCleary in its recent appearances in the tabloids.

According to them he'd been the victim in a sex scandal that involved the Baptist chaplain of his prison. "You are Dennis McLeary?" I asked needlessly.

"Yuh." He brightened.

"And I'm Deedee Murray, that three-year-old you saved from drowning. So, let's talk. Tell me why you enrolled here." That was normal procedure for Social Workers: Get A Prospect To Talk.

As with many recent jailbirds, Dennis longed for a real conversation. But first, he took long, deep breaths through his nose. He asked: "Is that per-foom ye' is wearin? Ain't smelled none since Nellie drenched herself with some to help fo' her to seduce me."

"Nellie being the girl with whom you had intercourse?" I nodded, having earlier ferreted out all the details. "Nellie Combbe, the daughter of the cook where you worked? Too young for you to make a plea of mutual consent. Her name was never revealed at your trial because your partner was only fourteen. You're alleging she seduced you?"

"Nah. Not to ye, Miss. It be just like with all them times I gits off, I'm part t'blame. Like when I gits t'leave parochial school sayin' a monk buggered me. I'd let him kiss me, enjoyed that. Hated wut followed. And after the accident wut killed my parents, when Mr. Blunt paid the fees for me to go to his Presbyterian Church's school and I gits buggered there by an Elder, I gits t'live in the big house by swearin' I keeps the Elder's secret. That Elder, he done offered me a box o' chocolates in exchange for takin' down my pants. I loves chocolates."

"You got out of prison three years early 'for good behavior.'"

"Weren't no 'good behavior.' I blackmailed that prison chaplain for buggerin' me. That's how I cut off servin' any more time."

"Good grief." I didn't want to listen to any more of what was basically a Confession. I couldn't give him the absolution. But after checking my watch to confirm he should get ten more minutes, I stood up to walk around my chair for a pause to think. I didn't go out the door. I reminded myself how this soiled man had saved my life, and I sat down on an armrest.

Dennis continued: "I'd had seventeen years o' bein' buggered in prison, mostly by the inmates. No good squealin' on none o' them. But, a Baptist chaplain wut drives a Cadillac? Done deal."

"Bugger? That term is foreign to me, I suppose it refers to homosexuality."

"Yuh. But I ain't no homo." He tried a hollow laugh. It was followed by a spate of dry coughs. "Just been in the wrong places, 'n I gits noticed 'cause o' the red hair. Yuh, 'n don't help that in Florida I's a registered sex offender."

"Have you ever thought of looking up Nellie, perhaps with the idea of marrying her?"

"Naw. Nellie's makin' good money as a cook in one o' them resort hotels. Mr. Blunt, he kept her on after the Mum died, and got Nellie the chef job. As for me, Mr. Blunt had made sure I learned how to chauffeur from old Terry, who lasted in the big house twenty years. When he turned down the offer to go with Mr. Blunt to Florida, I got his job, his clothes, and might have lasted if I hadn't screwed Nellie. After I gits sent to prison, fast forward five years 'n she gits married twice, and divorced twice. 'Curse of Florida,' a wife-killer told me. Wut about your Nanny. Where she be at?"

Terrible pain thrashed through me. Fraulein!

If I felt guilty about anything in my life, it was for not having screamed to my parents to not let Fraulein Hubmeyer leave us and go back to Austria. I stumbled over each word, wiping at fast-coming tears as I replied to Dennis's searing demand. "Fraulein returned home to Austria after Hitler's Anschluss. Austria's new Nazi bosses sent political dissidents to Concentration Camps. Fraulein's years in America brought her under suspicion. Why death? She attended a swimming meet where she scoffed and sneered at the suggestion that Adolf Hitler had been born in Austria. She'd left Europe before Hitler became famous: that's why Fraulein was unaware of the truth. Next morning, she was forced on to a train for the three day journey to Auschwitz and a gas chamber."

"Uh, even in prison us convicts heard about them gas chambers." Dennis sighed.

"Guess as our prisons weren't no Glory-Hallelujah joints but even so they wus still better than them."

"I was seventeen when I learned how she'd died. I learned too late. And any way it happened before I had enough money of my own to have traveled to Austria to bring her to Florida. But I certainly do blame myself for being too fixated on earning my BA from Barnard." Dabbing at my reddening eyes, I added: "I can't bear the guilt!"

I wept on, with huge balloon-like tears.

Dennis hated seeing a woman cry. The last time had been Nellie on his final day in that Florida courtroom, when he'd got his twenty-year sentence.

Now, he fiddled with the doorknob of my consulting room. He saw the corridor filling with Social Workers leading ex-convicts to the nearby room where tea and cookies were supplied. He gargled on his spit, and said: "Miss, let's us go on in with them others whose con-ver-sation hour's up. I like tea. 'N there's chocolate cookies in that room. I never lost wanting them, even though ours at Mr.Blunt's wus stale. I got wut was left over in the big house."

Drying my face, I forced out a question in line with the Social Worker policy of keeping a subject talking. "When did you go there?"

"I were six year old when I were taken up to live there by Mr. Blunt. My folks, thems had died. I were adopted. Never had had no cookies, nor no tea before."

I blew my nose, made a ball of the Kleenex, straightened my shoulders and turned off the lights of my allotted room.

Another bit of advice to prospective social workers had been: If An Ex-convict Makes A Wholesome Positive Suggestion Act On It Without Delay.

I followed Dennis to the tea and cookies.

Socializing in the room, I found myself face to face with an Episcopal minister who'd been a close friend of my father's. The Rev. Wilfrid Hanes was juggling a cup on its saucer when he approached me and asked: "And who is this?" He pointed his index finger at Dennis. "DeeDee, is this one of yours?"

I nodded carefully, judging this was not the day to advance Dennis on to a man wearing a priest's round collar.

Dennis, still too hungry for conversation, came into play on his own. A freckled hand went forward inviting the Reverend's plump fingers, one of which was adorned with a Harvard graduate's ring.

This Reverend didn't draw back. He accepted the invitation with an extremely strong handshake. "Yes, you are Dennis McLeary: I've read the newspaper accounts about you."

"None o'em true. Nellie's Mom wus tryin' to rip off Mr. Blunt. Noospappuhs loved how Mr. Blunt fought to win. Mom had no chance only 'cause Nellie weren't 'bout to declare nothin' in no court." Dennis stopped smiling. That was good thinking, because his teeth were as damaged as a cracked wall. He was in need of a first class dentist.

"I wasn't speaking of your trial," Father Hanes said gently.

"Uh, you meanin' when Nellie's Mom were hittin' Mr. Blunt for fifty thousand dollars. Had one o' 'em crooked Florida 'no win, no fee' lawyers. She sued sayin' Mr. Blunt shouldn't have had two adolescent kids "in puberty" under his roof; it were his fault Nellie lost her cherry. Judge ruled against Nellie's Mom. Her claim went nowheres when Nellie kept her mouth shut. I weren't lucky with my judge neither. Got twenty years in the slammer."

"I was referring to the rumpus over your recent claim that you had been abused by your prison's chaplain. Every priest must have followed it: that Baptist clergyman wanted to bring the case to the Supreme Court, to clear his name. But there's a centuries-old legal principle which bars lawsuits that involve the inner workings of religious groups."

The Reverend refilled his tea cup. Dennis helped himself to a fistful of Oreo cookies.

I put my own comment into what should have been a closed conversation: "The Florida Supreme Court decided not to hear the case after an appellate court threw it out. Have I got that correct?"

"Uh, yuh. More o' less. Chaplain got charged with 'two counts of lewd activity and ten counts of unlawful sexual acts. Them adds up to twelve felonies."

Judge refused him bail.

"Chaplin got booked into same prison where he'd buggered me."

Facing Father Hanes, I chirped: "Dennis told me he made a deal with the chaplain promising not to 'sing' if he could get three years shaved off his 1930 sentence. The chaplain leaned on his bishop, warning him that this case could open a pandora's box. In line with many Catholic bishops, this one agreed to a prompt burial of the situation. And after some threats for exposure to former victims now in Florida courts, the homosexual chaplain caved into Dennis's terms. So here we have Dennis as free as an uncaged bird."

There followed a quiet few minutes while we three finished drinking our tea.

The Reverend turned pensive.

He growled: "Sounds like a Roman Catholic priest's story. You don't hear so much about the Baptists or the Presbyterians sexually abusing members of their congregations."

I asked, "Father, do those two denominations have the biggest congregations?"

"They did, when counting all the splintered divisions. Then we Episcopalians took over to have the largest number of parishioners in the United States. But currently the Roman Catholics boast the greatest number."

Dennis bucked into the question. "I'd like to know more 'bout both o' 'em. What are them's differences?"

Solemnly, in a heavier tone, Father Hanes faced Dennis. "The most noticeable differences in the main denominations: Presbyterians and Baptists accept only two sacraments, Baptism, and Holy Communion, while we Episcopalians and the RCs practice seven Sacraments. Not much separates Episcopalians from Roman Catholics."

I broke in. "We have the Archbishop of Canterbury at the head of our church, the RCs have the Pope."

"Correct." The Reverend held tight to the conversation like an old time mariner hugging his mast. "But while both the

Episcopalians and the RCs all believe in the seven sacraments, there are considerable divisions to address."

"I wants t'hear. But wait. I wants t'git more tea." Dennis rushed to the elegant silver tray and refilled his cup from a large heavily engraved teapot: both provided by the university.

The Reverend studied his hand, was he thinking of how his hands handled Holy Communion in church? He said: "One important difference in particular fascinates me: the handling of money. On my own time I've been looking into the wealth of the Roman Catholic Church. And a totally unexpected thing caught my attention: one reason why the RC Church does not allow priests to marry is because among Episcopal and Eastern Orthodox Churches when a married priest dies his capital usually goes to his wife. While with the RC priests, unmarried and with no direct dependents, their capital usually goes to the church."

"Seems fair enough."

Hanes added "Also being celibate saves those priests from the demands and crises of family life, affording more time to concentrate on their calling."

Dennis inelegantly sucked saliva through his discolored teeth. "I'd like to know lots, lots more,"

Still speaking solemnly, without any spice from humor, Father Hanes suggested: "Come to the Cathedral of Saint John The Divine. It's only a few blocks from here. I work there with Bishop Manning. He's known for his helpful ideas. For evenings, he initiated several courses for interested parishioners: Ethics. Spiritual advancement. And we even have a class teaching better knowledge of English. That course exists in order to help immigrants find better jobs."

Dennis's face became transformed. From a sulky ex-convict's scowl he changed his expression to the electrified excitement of a formerly frustrated learner approaching a fulfilling horizon. "Sign me up for all three. Never went to no classes in prison, 'cause I'd been buggered by a teacher my first year."

I gave an unladylike grunt of relief, believing that Ethics, Spiritual Advancement and better use of the English language could all be beneficial for Dennis.

How could I have foreseen what trouble Dennis got into at the Cathedral?

St. John The Divine, the Episcopal Cathedral for the Diocese of New York City, had long been famous for its Halloween extravaganza.

During the twenty-five years of Bishop Manning's reign, the Halloween event accomplished several positive objectives. It magnetized an audience into its nave, and the cost of tickets contributed to the sum of twenty-five million dollars which the bishop hoped to raise before he ended his tenure.

Twenty-five million was the sum needed for completion of the cathedral, which had never been finished.

That aim propelled Bishop Manning into excessive efforts to reach the elusive twenty-five million. Among the several miscalculations were the extending of the festival to include people outside the congregation. Furthermore, the festival had vastly outgrown its beginnings of a lure for children to a better understanding of All Souls' Day, having developed now into a huge fracas of displaying expensive costumes, and provoking flirtatious comments among those who attended.

Said to be one of the largest cathedrals in the world, Saint John The Divine had the most impressive rose stained glass window in the United States.

It had one serious drawback: the very wealthy and social families had left the neighborhood. That was partly because Mrs. William Astor had built the grandest mansion in the city at 848 Fifth Avenue. Her ballroom could hold one thousand two hundred people, but the expression "the Four Hundred" was coined when the building was not yet completed and only four hundred could dine. It was far south past the length and breadth of Central Park, some blocks below where that park ends. Those wealthy families took their wallets with them. Their abandoned homes were replaced by slums, where low-income families and single mothers lived, the majority of them black. If they attended church, it was not at the Episcopal Cathedral.

The Cathedral did not stand alone. Columbia College, founded by England's King George III, had an imposing sweep of steps. Nearby was a later college for eventually-franchised women students:

Barnard. The entire campus embraced the title of Columbia University under the auspices of Nicholas Murray Butler. President Butler had a two-sided personality. Revered on campus, it was little known that when a Nobel Prize nominee poet arrived as a refugee from Occupied France to be interviewed for a professorship at Columbia, and was admitted into Butler's presence under his pen name, Butler threw him out after tearing up the contract where the poet had signed his real Jewish name.

There are world-class educational buildings in the same general area. Juilliard School of Music graces a sunny spot.

Not far away is the Union Theological Seminary which draws eminent scholars to pursue a BA in Religion and Theology. When Dennis learned that the School of Divinity—in addition to in-depth studies of the Bible accompanying practical skills— he felt intrigued until he heard that a

Master of Divinity degree depended upon a concentration in Chaplain ministry.

"Chaplain ministry? I thought I'd throw up." Dennis raged. "Remember, I was buggered by the chaplain of my prison."

Dennis had crossed the yards to my Social Work building. It is a very plain American contemporary-style place, never as attractive-looking as the imposing Theological Seminary manse, which—with its third floor arched windows—could be mistaken for a church.

Autumn had arrived. Most of the great old trees had shed their leaves, and they swirled like whipped cream in a bowl.

Some leaves stuck to my boots.

With the passing of months, Dennis had changed. Watching him sitting erect, no longer slouching, and with a pleased-with-himself grin on his face, I felt my hours with him had produced favorable results.

He'd lost his 'Florida-cracker' accent from the English lessons taught at St. John The Divine. He'd lost his belligerency. He'd lost his 'preyed upon orphan' look.

"Halloween's next week," he sang out, trilling like the migrant birds practicing outside my window for their southward flights. "Help me get the most gruesome costume. I want to be a ghoul."

I hated to discourage him. Ghouls at this event were for the very rich when the Cathedral had oil barons among the congregation.

When the Cathedral was begun, there had existed an up and coming social area along upper West Side Drive, overlooking the Hudson River. Decades later the Rockefeller family built a church there. That area had superseded Harlem, which had its heyday when the island belonged to Dutch settlers and was called New Amsterdam.

Dennis had absorbed a good deal of the place's history. He lived at a local YMCA, traveled by bus to his classes at the Cathedral, ate his meals at the corner drugstore and enjoyed the subway rides to Macy's on 34 Street to buy the few clothes he needed for New York's changes of season. He liked to think of himself as a New Yorker.

Florida was the rotten past.

He'd continued going to my Social Work twosome for conversations. I'd tried to help him economize, to save his remaining $13,000 principal. However, now when the huge extravaganza approached, Dennis wanted to spend a hefty sum wantonly on a seriously-expensive costume.

"No. Not a ghoul. You've never been to this Halloween event. You can't know that a big starring parade of ghouls starts it off. Grown-ups, not just teenagers and kindergarten kids."

"How about I go as some kind of animal? A fox, maybe, with a bushy tail."

"There'll be so many animals. I wouldn't recommend that."

Rev. Hanes came into my room. He'd made a habit of looking in when Dennis had his hour. I guess it was to check his progress, which had been terrific. The Reverend strode to my table and removed a thick telephone Directory. "Here, I heard your remark about costumes. Look in these Yellow Pages under costumes."

Dennis jumped at that suggestion. He thumbed through the pages under C.

Rev. Hanes continued: "Most revelers in the parade will have their heads covered with extremely elaborate whole-head masks. Costing hundreds of dollars. Left over from the days when very rich parishioners still lived in the neighborhood. A cloak could cost thousands."

I took over the Yellow Pages and drew my finger along Costumes. "Let's try this one: Theatrical. Second Hand. Conveniently near the 42 and Broadway subway stop."

Dennis didn't give up easily. "I could go as a little ghoul."

"No, no. This is an evening to bring children into the church. There will be dozens upon dozens of little ghouls." I locked up my designated room.

Rev. Hanes accompanied us to the nearest subway station. A wind had come up and it tore at my quilted jacket. My page-boy hairstyle lost its curl. When a cold sheet of rain swept the entrance to the subway, I was pleased to escape inside. Rev. Hanes didn't follow. He waved goodbye, separately, to each of us as if he didn't want Dennis to be connected to me.

The second hand theatrical costumes store was easy to find. It was tattered, grimy, and the salesgirl hadn't bothered to comb her hair, which fell to her waist. "What you want?"

I said, although it should have been unnecessary, "Costumes."

Dennis over-rode my answer. "Animal costumes. I could be an alligator, I'm from Florida."

"Too expensive for us to stock. No alligators, but bears start at $200."

In a stern voice, not to be tyrannized by this uncombed brat, I announced: "For me, along ago Queen's robe and crown. Not a penny over $100. For him, I like that Neptune outfit on the model there. Pay $50, for that."

The girl went to two racks and pulled out three elaborate gowns that could have been suitable for a queen of three or four centuries past. She reached toward a shelf for a selection of tiaras and crowns.

"Extra for a crown: $20."

"I'll take a tiara. Pay you $10 for that." I crossed the dusty floor to reach the King Neptune gold lamè pants and jacket. "Come and try this on," I called to Dennis.

"If I pay $50, you'll have to include the trident." he cautioned the salesgirl.

She removed the Neptune costume from the model, and grumpily handed it to Dennis. "It'll fit. Men's dressing rooms over there. Trident, $15 extra."

I'd decided to be Catherine de Medici, the Florentine Queen of France, best remembered as mother-in-law to Mary Queen of Scots. I thought my brown hair would suit a Florentine woman. The most extravagant gown for my money was in gold silk, tired but very regal, and matching Neptune's gold lamè. When I went to pay, I relented and took a crown instead of a tiara, and gave the girl her extra $10.

Dennis sounded ecstatic with his choice. "Neptune, King of the Sea. How about that?

I wish Nellie could have seen me in that dressing room! I promise you I'm going to wow everyone in the Halloween procession. This is the life, all right." At the cash register he shoved out the $50, and without a grudge added $15 for his trident.

The salesgirl stopped us at the door. She'd forgotten to get a $100 deposit against loss or damage to our four items. In addition, she pressed a piece of burlap over the trident's sharp teeth. "You don't want to kill anybody with it," she snapped.

Her sour dismissal couldn't dampen Dennis's joyous mood. I'd never seen him dance, but as we caught up with the five o'clock human traffic flooding into the subway, he was prancing like a young deer.

October 31st dawned bright and cheerful, when it would have been more appropriate for All Souls' Day if the skies were darkened to a grey and the wind bitter.

Costumed participants in the Cathedral's extravaganza were being admitted by a side door. I'd qualified as a regular member of the congregation and had added Dennis's name as "a friend."

As Dennis and I crushed our way through the side entrance we could see the long queue of hopefuls pushing shoulders to get inside the Cathedral to grab the few available seats.

The event had been nearly sold-out for a month.

A black night conveniently fell by seven p.m., contrasting with the long light summer nights of a few months earlier.

Watching the first monster-like performers leaning into the occupied pews, playfully scaring the small children into subdued shrieks, I remembered that I'd intended to put on make-up to try to have my plain face match the beauty of my queenly robe.

I excused myself and found a nearby ladies room properly labeled: "Powder

Room". There I applied generous amounts of foundation, eyebrow color, and rouge. I finished off the look with generous amounts of scarlet lipstick. I wanted to get into the spirit of the event by making my lips look as if I'd been drinking blood.

Dennis, who'd been waiting quietly, still in his exhilarated state, rejoined me with a huge grin and we found a place where the main parade had started to move. The most fearsome ghouls had done their weaving with those traditional faltering steps that imitated ships fighting against heavy seas.

This King Neptune proceeded to adapt into the role of ruler of the oceans. He took on a majestic stance, while removing the cover from his trident. He would have used an imposing stride, but a sixteen-year-old boy in a rabbit costume yelled at him:

"Ouch, you jerk! You could've broken my toe. You've ripped off the left rabbit foot."

Dennis looked down at the torn off rabbit foot.

He reverted to the subdued convict he'd been. "Sorry. I can fix that. King Neptune doesn't need gloves and I've got two on my belt. I can cut off the glove's pinky finger. And I've got safety pins."

The boy hesitated for an instant. He took his time to examine Neptune's gloves. "Okay."

"Come on, we can go to the Men's Room. Just push your way through this mob."

"Bill!" A shout interrupted Dennis's offer.

A middle-aged newcomer, also wearing a rabbit costume, elbowed a path through the moving horde. He grabbed the sixteen-year-old's right arm and like a Caterpillar truck, towed him to the Men's Room.

Nonplused, Dennis delayed while thinking through his role in what had happened.

He was swept along with the main pageant. I'd witnessed the destruction of the costumed foot of the first rabbit. But I was otherwise occupied by the time the adult rabbit appeared on the scene.

Costumed as Robin Hood's jolly Friar Tuck, a character so often part of May Games' Festivals, a jovial stranger had pressed himself against me, although we were both trying to go with the flow of the crowd around us.

"Can't say I'm sorry," he joked across a woman's shoving shoulder. "Quickly, my name's Hal Pierce. Tell me yours so I can find you again."

I looked at this modern day Friar Tuck, and felt glad to see that his stomach was a pad that had somehow slipped around towards his back. I've never taken any interest in fat men. "Deedee Murray," I called, while two fake nuns tried to get between us.

Hal wasn't having any of the nuns' guile. He managed to regain a position next to me and held on to it until we were well down the Cathedral nave.

I'd lost sight of Dennis. Hal was emerging from Friar Tuck. I liked the sound of Hal's voice, the lilt of his laugh, and the caring sparkle in his eyes.

Dennis never made it to the nave.

Memories of the childhood abuses and seventeen years of being sodomized in prison catapulted Dennis to follow Bill to the Men's Room, although he had to fight the costumed horde very roughly to get there.

He opened the Men's Room door to see what he'd dreaded: both rabbit costumes lay discarded on the tile floor and he saw the middle-aged man sodomizing sixteen-year-old Bill.

Without a word, he removed the piece of burlap and plunged his trident's three deadly teeth into a fold of fat in the middle-aged man's back.

Hideous screams from pain mixed with rage resounded against the bathroom's tiles.

These were followed by loud shouts: "Call an ambulance. Bill, call the police!"

Bill scrambled to retrieve his rabbit costume, and put it on, before he replied: "If I call an ambulance, you won't tell what's happened! Promise, you won't tell. My father could…"

"Police?" Dennis repeated, questioning. As if it had been a fire alarm, now Dennis was alert to his own peril.

Was this incident going to send him back to prison?

Bill turned toward Dennis: "That's my algebra teacher, he—"

"Police!' Dennis repeated, prepared to bolt before the boy finished. Tearing out the trident's teeth from the sodomizer's back, he broke the trident into four sections, then threw the pieces along with the top half of his King Neptune outfit into an outside bin.

Lancing himself into the bustling crowd, he fled back to the side entrance making his way through the thinning arrivals.

Outside the Cathedral a friendly hand briefly stopped him. A familiar voice matched it. Rev. Hanes said, sounding disturbed: "Dennis, what are you up to? Is Deedee on her own inside? What happened to the top of your costume?"

"Uh. Got to go… Deedee's okay. Sorry. Sorry!" Dennis pushed the hand free and sped zigzag like a fox from hunters to reach the subway station.

He had correct change for the turnstile, hurried to the south bound trains' platform, and waited.

There were a few curious stares from other would-be passengers who were waiting, and one child pointed a finger in a rude gesture.

The child sneered to her mother: "Lucky we didn't make it into the Halloween extrava-ganza, if that costume's like what we'd have seen."

There were no remarks aimed at him when he reached his YMCA's lobby.

He offered none. Dennis went upstairs to dig under his bed for an oversized duffle bag and proceeded to pack his scarce possessions into it. After cutting up the pants of his King Neptune costume, he flushed the pieces down the hallway's toilet and returned to his closet.

Dennis chose to pack clothes for contrasting climates: T-shirts and thick sweaters. These he'd placed at the bottom of his five-foot-long duffle bag. Now he hid his passport and ready money deeper under the briefs. He had no trinkets or photographs to safekeep from the five months he'd been out of prison.

Stripping the bed and topping the used sheets with his used towels, he then ferreted out an envelope. He went down to the lobby to pay his outstanding account, then placed a one hundred dollar bill into the envelope to recompense Deedee's insurance loss to the second-hand-costumes' theater-district store against damage or loss.

"If a lady called Deedee Murray comes asking for me, give her this envelope. And thanks for everything." He gave a fake military salute; military, in hopes this night-clerk would judge him ex-military rather than an ex-convict.

The night temperature had dropped. He fished out a warm jacket from the duffle bag and hit the streets while figuring out which subway would take him to the docks where some maritime companies offered jobs. He was hoping to find a ship so hurried to fill a need that there would be no back checking before today's sailing.

He slept on a Battery Park bench on top of his duffle bag. By nine in the morning he'd found a shipping company with its door open.

⏣

Chapter 3

November 1, 1947 RMS DEVERON and Kusadasi, Turkey

Dennis McLeary lay in his upper bunk in the waiters' hall aboard the Clan Line's RMS DEVERON. Crowding him, taking up half the bunk was his oversized duffle bag.

He'd pulled up the duffle bag to the far side, in hopes of protecting his passport and money from thieves and himself from being buggered.

The reason he'd been banished to his bunk was because during his initial appearance as a waiter at lunch he'd dropped a tray full of whiskey glasses. The whiskey had been spilled, the glasses were smashed.

He couldn't be fired. The ship had passed Sandy Hook, and dispatched its pilot. But he could foresee a cut in wages.

His bunks buddy, an Egyptian Muslim called Ahmed Rashid, proved very talkative in his careful use of English. "Dennis, you will not be chastised further. My last bunks companion, also Muslim, died in the Infirmary today and must be buried at sea within twenty-four hours. You will go to the funeral. Show respect by attending Seth's burial. We have many Muslims aboard who will appreciate that. You will make friends. Cohorts."

"What did Seth die of?"

"Tuberculosis."

"And I'm on his mattress? If so, I want another mattress." Dennis recalled a cell mate he'd had during his first year in jail, who had died of that disease, and he had been warned it was highly contagious.

With some difficulty Dennis eased out of the bunk to stand upright next to the bunk. He had kept one hand on his duffle bag, that had remained in the bunk. "Do I go to the Head Steward to ask for another mattress?"

"No. Allah be praised, our bunks were sanitized very early after he died. Dennis, you do not want to approach the Head Steward. Keep well away! I would wish to be given a preventive from catching the disease, but I cannot chance his displeasure. As the Prophet taught, we are in the hands of Allah. I am not afraid of the disease for myself, but I would never forgive the Chief Steward if I gave the disease to my wife."

Dennis found enough space to make a half turn. He didn't want Ahmed to see his expression of relief! The fact he was married and said to love his wife reduced favorably any chance that Ahmed would turn out a buggerer. "Been married long?"

"As long as I have been at sea. My adored Fila came from a family who would not give her in marriage to an unemployed man. It is my sorrow that to make money I must be apart from her most of every year."

"So what's your job on the DEVERON?"

"I shove coal. You must forgive me that my fingernails are so filthy black. With my former bunk's mate spitting blood in our basin, I did not wash as often as I should have."

Prompted by his remark, Ahmed crossed to the six inch diameter basin to use a nail brush.

Seconds later he pulled a prayer rug from under the bottom bunk, knelt toward Mecca, and proceeded to pray.

A knock on the door advised that his former bunks mate was about to be lowered into the sea.

Ahmed replaced his prayer rug, pulled out a small suitcase, removed his best clothing, changed from pajamas to jacket and trousers and over those pulled over a djellaba, and led Dennis through the ship to the service.

On arriving, Ahmed joined a group of fellow Muslims who collectively washed Seth's naked body. Dry, he was wrapped in a cotton sheet, then placed on a door-like plank while the ship's Captain Igleton read from the Koran in Arabic.

Ahmed approved of his pronunciation. He danced his head up and down, but he refrained from attempting to shake his captain's hand.

Dennis felt that Captain Igleton had privately given him a thorough inspection, although careful not to make a show of it.

Prayers over, the sheet-hidden corpse was positioned on the plank and slowly lowered into a rough sea.

Dennis wanted to make a quick retreat, but a smiling Ahmed delayed him on the deck. "Next time you attend a service on board the DEVERON, maybe it will be for the captain to marry you."

"And he could?" Surprised, Dennis— who had earlier compared Captain Igleton to Correction Officers in Florida he remembered had abused him—took a second look at his captain. He studied him with the same intensity with which he'd studied books in Columbia University's library. He altered his original assessment, and decided to like him.

Hitching up the cuffs of his trousers to descend the employees' stairs to their stark quarters below, Dennis asked himself if he could ever marry after having been buggered so many times.

At the DEVERON'S second port of call, Dennis got permission—along with ten of the ship's other personnel—to swim off a beach near Kusadasi, in Turkey.

The November weather was warmer there than in New York City, but the

Mediterranean's water held on to the colder night temperatures.

Dennis had reckoned on cold water and brought a sweater to team with his T-shirt and jeans. At the beach, eight of the group decided against a swim and to tour the local ruins of Ephesus, founded in 1100 B.C.

Mehmet, a fellow waiter aboard the DEVERON, who had made friendly-type overtures to Dennis after Seth's funeral, said: "Over those hills is Ephesus. You could see ancient buildings there that rival those of Greece. Big trading post in its day. Still lures the big spenders, like those of Saudi Arabia. From the Roman era, it has an arena for gladiators, a huge fort, and a house that is said to be where your St. Mary lived her last years. I'm taking the tour. Want to come?"

"No, thanks. I'd rather take a swim off the beach down below." Dennis waved off Mehmet.

Looking beyond the DEVERON group's bus, he caught sight of a cluster of changing rooms at the bottom of steps leading to the beach. He stared at them, intrigued to watch three Muslim girls in abaya Moslem cover-ups as they entered—each one separately— into a changing room.

Minutes later, he was amazed to see the three girls emerge wearing very revealing two-piece bathing suits.

In this Muslim country? Here, where some women still wore the hijab to hide their faces and bodies?

On the road from their ship's dock in Kusadasi, his bus had passed four elderly women wearing the hijab, which covered them totally leaving only their eyes visible. Why had these young women worn hijabs, here, in modernized Turkey?

The three girls were very different. One had black hair, and a plump hairy body. Even from a distance her legs seemed black due to the abundance of hair on them. She was very tall—pushing six feet—an extra large person, and singularly unattractive.

Next to her, running like a greyhound in a race, sped a girl with russet red hair. She was short, under five feet, and very pretty although abnormally thin. The contrast with her companion was dramatic.

The third girl trailed behind these two, limping: a cripple. She had mud-colored hair, cut short. In her two-piece bathing suit her breasts bobbed like apples in a bucket game.

Dennis hurried down the stairs to pay for a changing room.

When Dennis reached the shoreline all three girls were already swimming. In the water their athletic know-how also contrasted sharply. The tall black haired girl was the slowest, treading timidly. The crippled girl had a sad little dog-paddle action.

It was the red head who ended competing with Dennis, doing an Australian crawl that could have had a place in the Olympics.

Finally, out of breath and treading, she welcomed Dennis's arrival next to her: "Hi," she pushed out between gasps for air. Her accent was American, without any trace of Turkish.

"Hi," Dennis gave back, also treading but not gasping. "I'm Dennis. You're local here?"

"Yes. I live in Ephesus. My name? It's rather ordinary: Myriam. Mother's from here, my Dad is from Saudi Arabia, but has made me live with him in New York when he was advising part of the Saudi Delegation to the UN." She ran out of air, and took three large gulps. "You're quite a swimmer!"

"So are you, Myriam. Let's head for those rocks, but keeping as far out as we are now."

"Fine!" She kicked with a fountain-like spray and reached out her left arm.

A leftie? He very much liked that they were both red-heads and lefties.

Myriam's two companions began screaming at her. They might have used four-letter words like Merde. Dennis had heard it often. It had been every second word spoken by a French Canadian prisoner in his jail back in Florida. Now he reckoned that Myriam's companions weren't from a religious background.

At their next breathing stop, Dennis asked: "You're Muslim?"

"Yes. But My mommy's quite opposed to all the strict demands put on Saudis. I think that's why she's divorced from my father. He's Wahhabi, meaning he's austerely puritanical. He believes in the principle of 'enjoining good and forbidding wrong.' Ouch!"

"Uh. Tough on you?"

"I was kept in his apartment all the time. I could go to see the news at TRANSLUX, but never go to a real movie! My father practices Salafism. That means he doesn't permit any modernizations that deviate from the early teachings of Mohammed the Prophet."

Myriam took new gulps of air, and with a solemn expression swam to be parallel with the far rocks.

Dennis followed. At the point where they had agreed to return towards the beach, Dennis suddenly stopped, grew vertical and gently pulled Myriam's shoulders to touch his – and kissed her on the lips. RAPTURE!

She responded with matching passion, sucking his lips into her mouth.

The wondrous kiss was interrupted by hysterical screeches from the two women waiting for Myriam on the beach.

M yriam pulled away from Dennis. Also treading vertically, she whispered—although there was no one but Dennis to hear her: "The tall one's my fiance's aunt. Never married. Too tall. Too hairy. She was supposed to chaperone me on what was described as a private beach for women only. But my mother knew better: she's had her flirtations on this beach."

"How come you're living with your mother now?'"

"Under the terms of her divorce she gets me six months every year."

"When's the wedding?"

"Not while I'm with my mother. She'd never comply with all those old traditions for a Muslim marriage. And that horrible man would have to net me first, which I'd never let happen. I'll only marry a man I truly love."

The tall woman left the beach and began to swim towards Myriam and Dennis.

Dennis asked: "Can that woman swim well enough to catch us?"

"Uh, no. She couldn't. Not if we go out to the cove where the waves are wilder. Come on. Follow me."

At their next hidden spot, he queried: "You getting married soon?"

"I certainly hope not. I can't stand the man. According to his precepts my father let me peek at him through lattice work on our terrace. Terribly selfish-looking. He'd never give me a tasty kiss like you did. Just wants a baby-making machine. No kissing involved." Myriam cautioned Dennis: "You stay far out in the sea. My chaperone can't swim very well, big as she is. I won't get punished with anything worse than a verbal beating. She won't dare tell I've been kissed. She'd never get to go to a beach again."

"And the other woman? The one with the mousey hair?"

"She doesn't count for anything. She tells so many lies that no one believes her if she's telling the truth. Dennis, come back here tomorrow. Same time, Same place."

"Depends. Depends if my ship's still undergoing repairs." Dennis swam near

Myriam, always well behind but not out of earshot. "Our ship was supposed to make an ordinary delivery of grain, but damage was discovered. It's being fixed. Could take a week."

"I'll be here. I want to be kissed more by you." Like a racing car she bolted for the finish line.

At the beach she didn't turn or make any sign to him. His eyes, blinking now as a new wind whipped up waves that hit him in the face, Dennis watched the changing rooms until she emerged. He could make her out from her companions because she was much smaller, and because she had a jaunty walk. The three disappeared into a pre-World War II Chevrolet. The car had its rear windows blackened to hide the occupants.

The following day, right on time, but with two different companions, Myriam appeared in front of the beach's changing rooms. She was sandwiched between two older women wearing abayas, which they discarded in their separate cabins. They emerged as Twentieth Century flappers. These ladies were showing off their emancipation by sporting slacks and see-through blouses. One woman had chosen scarlet lipstick and fingernail polish to complete her Westernized image.

Neither of these companions intended to swim. They'd brought no towels or swimsuits.

Myriam had arrived in the brown dress favored by some unmarried Moslem girls. It was in the same style as what she'd worn the day before, when she'd been covered with the hijab. She'd hurried into her changing room. Like with the speed of a military missile, she'd been fast to rid herself of the ugly brown dress. Without a word to Dennis, Myriam ran to the shoreline in her two piece bathing outfit and dove into the Mediterranean.

Dennis chose to simulate indifference. He found another nearby cove to swim diagonally in Myriam's wake.

Around the cove's distinctive high rocks, Myriam and Dennis resumed their intimate kissing. This time Myriam thrust her tongue into Dennis's mouth so far that it touched the deepest part of his throat.

The cool water around them was like a sweet sauce on forbidden fruit.

When Myriam drew away to take deep breaths, instead of returning her lips to his, she murmured: "My wedding dress arrived from Saks Fifth Avenue this morning. Sent by my father: he even included the red sash I'm to wear from my shoulder to the waist and from there to my hem to show I'm a virgin. Dennis, listen to me; I don't want to marry anyone but you!"

She'd spoken so shyly that the words were almost obliterated by the sound of the sea's waves.

Startled, supremely happy yet anxious, Dennis said, loud enough to blanket any other noise: "Myriam, I LOVE YOU and I want to marry you. But I don't know how we can make that happen before you're forced into marriage with the monster!"

"Take me with you when the DEVERON sails."

"Myriam, my wonderful brave darling, I'm not a passenger on the ship. I'm a very low level employee. I haven't had a chance to tell you about myself, but—"

"No buts. My mother tracked down all the info I'd want. She knows you came on board to work as a waiter in the passengers' dining room. You'd given your address as the Union Theological Seminary, and stated you'd decided to quit your studies to see the world. You have very little savings, and preferred to work in a humble job rather than to go as a paying passenger."

"That's what I told the Maritime Offices, but it's not true and I don't want to keep the truth from you. I'd been in prison for the last seventeen years and was on the Columbia University campus not studying Theology but to go to a Social Worker for help in coping with life on the outside. No help there getting employment. My job before I went into the clink had been as a chauffeur. Now, after the war, chauffeurs were not in demand."

"Mother never found out why you went to prison. Don't tell me if you don't want to."

"I want to ,now. No secrets between us. I had sex with a girl whose mother worked for my employer. She was fourteen, I was four years older. In Florida THERE'S A LAW AGAINST HAVING SEX WITH GIRLS UNDER EIGHTEEN. Can't claim she'd initiated it. That doesn't work in Florida. My sentence? Twenty years. I was listed as a Sexual Offender."

"Twenty years? I thought you said 'seventeen.'"

Dennis paused. There would be no further running-brook-like rush of words. Searing pain always accompanied memories of being sodomized. To gain time to describe what had happened, he stretched out on his back and let the cold Mediterranean prepare him to reveal his life's worst experiences. "I'd been buggered since I was a kid in parochial school; my confessor did me when I was preparing for Holy Communion. I stopped believing in most of what was in the catechism. At my next school, a Presbyterian one, it was an Elder of the local church. Huh, so much for their Predestination theory. When I was in jail, there were gangs that held me down while they did it to me. But it was the prison chaplain that buggered me until I traded my silence for three years off my sentence for 'good behavior.' I didn't squeal. That explains the seventeen years instead of twenty."

"Oh dear, dear Dennis. I'm weeping so hard, listening to this. How can I bear it?" Myriam dived below water to position her tiny body under his, and held her breath while she clasped her arms around his waist. She kissed his chest, his neck, his upper arms.

Dennis turned around to make their stomachs touch and drew her up to gulp air. He said: "We'll get married on the DEVERON. It's only a matter of smuggling you on board once you've shaken off your chaperone. Myriam, how tall are you?"

"Not as tall as you. Nowhere near. I'm four feet eleven inches, and that's all of me."

"Do you think you could fit into a sixty-inches-long duffle bag?"

"Five feet long! I'll make sure I do."

"Ship's been repaired. Sails tomorrow afternoon once it has stowed the cargo."

"Meet me at the Grand Emporium in Kusadasi. I'll use a changing room in the store to do the trick. I'll bring my favorite auntie who'll fit into my abaya while I get into your duffle bag. Two o'clock all right?" Myriam called back, heading around the cove for shore, "Be sure to bring a friend to help carry the duffle bag, I weigh more than you think."

At noon the next day Dennis asked Mehmet, his friend from Seth's funeral, to help him. Ahmed had begged off when he heard about Myriam's plan: "I can't take a chance on losing my job. My wife has found an apartment for sale in Cairo. Where we can make a down payment."

Mehmet said: "Allah be praised. Ahmed, count your blessings. I have been looking for six years for a reasonable apartment so my fiancèe and I can get married. Haven't found one I could afford." Mehmet, dreaming of a romantic adventure to boast about when smoking his hookah, quickly agreed to join up. But there followed the regular interruption of the Muezzins' call for that day's third prayers. Both men pulled out their rugs and knelt.

Dennis used the interruption to juggle ideas.

When Mehmet stood up, Dennis suggested: "Let's say you want to go to the Grand Emporium to buy sheets and towels for your new apartment. Say you're moving in as soon as the DEVERON reaches Alexandria. You've brought a duffle bag to carry them. But you'll put Myriam into the duffle bag, if she can't manage that by herself. You'll need some kind of help moving the duffle bag, once she's in it."

Mehmet delayed giving his reply. Finally, he asked: "Have you got any money?"

After seventeen years in prison, Dennis had learned to say little as regarded money.

Silently, Dennis lifted down his duffle bag and emptied it of all its contents. He positioned the clothing under his mattress but tucked his passport and cash into his ready wallet. He muttered: "Some money. I can request more when we offload Myriam in Alexandria. Can't wire from the DEVERON. Come on, Mehmet, let's go find the Grand Emporium."

Armed with legal papers for disembarkation, Dennis and Mehmet plunged into the quiet nap-time peculiar to early afternoons in Muslim countries.

Kusadasi's customary crowds, except for a group of gaping tourists, had emptied Kusadasi for home and bed. Profiting by the city's quiet time, Mehmet and Dennis hurried to the Grand Emporium, where they located Myriam in the ladies accessories section.

Myriam stood alone, unchaperoned, near flocks of handbags. She was wearing an abaya.

Nearby were fitting rooms.

A middle-aged woman came out of one of them ostensibly to select a handbag to match a dress for Myriam. She held high a printed rayon shift on a hanger.

She said in heavily accented English, "Come inside my fitting room and try on the dress to see how it looks, and if it fits I 'll buy it for you." That was the cue to announce Dennis's appearance.

Myriam, quick to realize that Dennis had arrived with his friend and was carrying the duffle bag, headed for the fitting room.

Dennis, playing an anxious husband searching for a gift for his wife, waited to push the duffle bag under the door that separated him from Myriam. He was waiting for a changing of the guard of the salesgirls.

At the same time as a new saleslady appeared, a very old woman emerged from the fitting rooms. She was as short as Myriam, under five feet and that height seemed less due to osteoporosis. Bent over like a pecking bird, she had the tiny steps of a person dying of Parkinson's disease. She was wearing Myriam's burka.

Myriam had managed to position herself into Dennis's duffle bag.

Within seconds this old woman was followed out by Myriam's chaperone, who brought the Emporium's selected dress and handbag. She placed these on a counter and pulled out a wallet to pay for them, adding a spate of rapid Turkish Arabic orders.

These two women left the store, once the dress and handbag were wrapped.

Dennis could see through the Grand Emporium's windows that a limousine collected them and sped away.

Mehmet then brought into play his Near Eastern guile. Adding his own spate of Turkish, he ended being taken to the changing rooms and being given a trolley in which to push "his duffle bag full of towels for his wedding'".

Dennis stopped a passing taxi and helped Mehmet lift the duffle bag into a passenger seat. When the two men arrived at DEVERON's gangway, they borrowed a ship's transport dolly to move the duffle bag and its very precious cargo to the waiters' accomodations. There, together, they raised the duffle bag into Dennis's bunk.

Not until "lights out" did Myriam push open the duffle bag's top to get more air than had been provided by Dennis's minutely pierced holes. She wiggled her head and chest out of the duffle bag, but due to the extremely narrow space of Dennis's bunk she'd been unable to release her legs.

No complaints from Abdul. He had transferred himself to the Sick Bay, saying he had fallen and was afraid" "HE'D GOT INTERNAL INJURIES."

Clever Abdul. He'd managed to extricate himself from the Dennis-and-Myriam human smuggling situation while opening the possibility of medical leave in Egypt which would give him time with his wife.

With no false modesty, Myriam said: "I've got to go to the bathroom."

Dennis repositioned the duffle bag for its bottom to rest on the floor and gently released Myriam.

Outside the sleeping quarters he led her down the silent corridor that offered a bare sign: TOILETS.

Keeping guard as purposefully as a Grenadier outside Buckingham Palace until Myriam came back out into the corridor, Dennis thought carefully how he should proceed that night alone with Myriam.

Even while believing they could be married in the morning, Dennis belted himself sternly. He determined not to get labeled a "sex offender" again. He hung on the side of Ahmed's bunk to stretch his head up to give a good night kiss. Then Dennis left Myriam alone in his own bunk to sleep, still a virgin.

The ship was well underway to its next port of call, Alexandria, when Myriam went to DEVERON's captain with a request that the two could be married by him.

Myriam had already gone to the acting-Purser to pay for a cabin that had been vacated by two New Yorkers who had left the ship at Kusadasi.

Romantically inclined, forever wishing he could have a wedding night, the acting-Purser accepted Myriam's thin story of having been left behind aboard ship when her chaperone heard the final gong to "leave ship" but she had not due to being in a bathroom.

At least that tale covered the reason why she had no luggage.

The captain was no easy romantic. He had worked his way up through the Clan Line, holding every job from lieutenant up, plying oceans from India and South

Africa. Founded in India in 1876, this was a busy shipping company that had helped the British army to be supplied from the Boer War through World War II. In its later years some ships had carried twelve paying passengers.

He received Myriam in his office, well designed to hold trophies from the many countries he had visited. Gruffly, but with a trace of kindliness, he listened in a gentlemanly manner to Myriam's plea. He had not remained seated, but had stood up from his elaborate carved-in-India chair when she entered. He knew a lady when he saw one.

"Please sit down. May I call you Miss Myriam? May I offer you a glass of sherry? Tell me, do you happen to have your passport with you?" From her New York accent and America-bought clothes, he'd assumed she was from the United States.

"How d'you do? Yes, my first name is Myriam. I do have my passport. Here it is. No sherry, thank you."

The captain's sparse eyebrows raised toward a tanned forehead. He felt surprised to recognize a Saudi Arabian passport. Scanning it quickly, he was relieved to see that Myriam was twenty-one-years old. He said, weighing each word solemnly: "The DEVERON is registered in Bermuda, therefore I am legally permitted to perform marriages on board my ship. You are of legal age to be married without parental consent. But as you are from Saudi Arabia, there could be a difficulty that—"

Hurling good manners aside, Myriam swiftly interrupted the captain: "Sir, I live with my mother. She has been divorced from my father for many years, and she has given me her blessing to be married on board this ship to Dennis McLeary."

"Dennis McCleary? He is a waiter on board my ship, but hired by the port office before the New York police scoured through foreign ships that were in New York harbor the day we sailed. He is an ex-convict."

"Dennis served enough years to be re-admitted to society."

"He lied to our port office. Told them he was a Divinity student at the Union Theological Seminary."

"Dennis was on the Columbia University campus as an ex-convict needing the help of a Social Worker."

"I presume he smuggled you on board. For that, he will be fired. There may be charges against him launched by the New York police for having physically injured a Mr. Gangden, an algebra teacher, who may press charges."

"Dennis caught that algebra teacher in the ACT OF SODOMIZING A SIXTEEN-YEAR-OLD boy."

"I wasn't aware of the circumstances." The captain put his hands together. His fingers mimicked a chapel with two doors. He opened his thumbs to an empty fleshy nave. "As the captain of a ship I have had problems with men sodomizing each other. You may call Dennis McLeary. I will study your request."

Dennis was received politely but not cordially. He produced his passport. The captain said:"I will be your marriage officer. I will register the marriage. But you must confirm all the paperwork in Alexandria in front of a local judge."

The captain produced a Bible and a copy of the Koran from a drawer in his desk. "You must pay two hundred and sixty five pounds to the Bermuda Registry of Marriages. Here, place a palm on the holy book of your choice... Dennis do you take Myriam as your lawfully wedded wife?"

Dennis's right hand hovered over first the Bible, then over the Koran, and settled on the Bible. "I do."

"Myriam do you take Dennis as your lawfully wedded husband?" She kissed the Koran, then whispered: "I do."

"I now pronounce you man and wife," the captain rushed the words, and crossed the room where he poured sherry into three crystal glasses. "I need a drink…"

Myriam put out a hand for hers. "And I want one too, but first: aren't you going to give Dennis permission to kiss the bride?"

"Dennis McLeary, you may kiss your bride," the captain acted promptly on Myriam's—not Dennis's—suggestion, in a mock-scolding voice.

Dennis drew Myriam into his arms, but their long meaningful kiss was less passionate than the ones they had glorified in off the Kusadasi beach. This was a tender kiss.

Finally pulling away, Dennis said sadly: "I didn't get a chance to buy a ring for you."

"I'll pick one out in Alexandria," Myriam sang out. "And you'll have to forget I wore this awful brown dress, the one I go shopping in when I leave my mother's house. Turkish Muslim unmarried girls wear unflattering brown. Probably not to ignite the wrong feelings in men they meet."

"The right feelings," Dennis smiled, and seemed happier about the conditions of their wedding. No wedding gown, no ring.

Captain Igleton gave Myriam a tired geranium plant in its pot, removing it from his desk. "I bought this in Barcelona. You must have flowers: this one will have to do." He kissed her hand and opened his cabin's door with a bow to her. For Dennis, he held up the all-important wedding certificate.

The Purser and Mehmet were called in to sign the certificate as witnesses.

Sherry, passed all around, was ignored by Mehmet, but accepted by newly liberated Myriam.

When Mehmet left to look for a rug to join others of the Muslims in evening prayers, Myriam asked the Purser for the key to her stateroom. The Purser blushed, his eyes rolling with sexual excitement.' Key in hand, it was Myriam who led the way to her marital bed.

Her door closed, she unbuttoned Dennis's clothes, then slipped out of her ugly brown dress and modest silk slip for them to stand together naked. They made love: they didn't need a bed.

Chapter 4

Alexandria, Egypt

From the DEVERON's deck, Alexandria looked beautifully white and pure. Dennis could not see the sewage overflowing on the streets. He could not hear the screams of starving children. He could not smell the rotting sores of the lepers. Mehmet, once they had got ashore their separate ways, his face radiant, led them to meet his fiancée. "It is my turn to be married," he sang out.

His fiancée, Iliana, was waiting beside a filled-up bus. She was fat, at least thirty, and wore the hijab headscarf according to Muslim tradition. She did not cover herself with a burqa.

She acted very obedient to Mehmet and he continued to glow with happiness.

With no space for them on the bus, Mehmet made a grand gesture to hail a taxi. "Cost the same as four of us on the bus," he explained sheepishly.

It took them to the nearby Hastings Street shopping area, where Myriam and Dennis bought bathing suits and beach towels.

Laughing, Myriam said, showing off her newly liberated self, "We don't need any sleep wear!"

Dennis, unsmiling, with straight lips, cut off any more similar remarks. "You need a wedding ring. There's a jewelry counter. You pick out which one appeals to you."

Myriam chose the cheapest gold plated unadorned circlet, pushing out the third finger of her right hand.

Dennis gave it a playful slap, caught up her left hand, and placed the ring on the third finger there. "In America, we use the left hand."

"Left hand, right hand, as a Muslim, I shouldn't be wearing a ring at all. Let's go for a swim!"

Mehmet interrupted. "You need to place an announcement in the local paper that you got married on the DEVERON. You need to send that two hundred and sixty-five pounds to the Bermuda Marriage Bureau. I'll take you to the newspaper office. I'll take you to where you can send a cable to your American bank. Otherwise, ring or no ring, you will not be legally married."

Dennis acted on both suggestions, which he followed by hosting a meal for Mehmet and Ili at a beachside café. After months on the DEVERON, Mehmet had double helpings of the café's local seafood, thanking Dennis three times as if he was at prayers.

When they left the café, Mehmet paid for a changing tent at the nearest beach where

Dennis and Myriam could try out their new bathing suits and safely leave their clothes, watches and money under lock and key.

This beach sprawled like Islam's symbolic crescent moon all the way to the Celex Bay dolphin point.

Hand in hand, Dennis and Myriam frolicked down to the bay's edge. Together they dove into the gentle waves. Together they swam far out beyond the sight of any beachgoers or long-range swimmers.

Dennis, not consciously beginning a ballet, took Myriam's slight body to hold its entire four feet eleven inches' length over his head, twirled it, tossed it up a yard, then dropped it to the ocean's surface. As if she was a professional ballerina, Myriam acted out the postures and arm stretches of a true replica of Swan Lake's early scene: a thing of exquisite beauty.

Myriam finally broke away to swim farther out. She removed her new bathing suit, hooked the straps on her left arm, and welcomed Dennis with her right.

They made love, savoring wonderful joy!

In his ecstasy, Dennis had lost hold of his hurriedly-taken-off swimming trunks and they had floated westward.

Too wonderfully enthralled, Dennis followed the trunks westward. Myriam followed him. Together they swam toward a magnificent sunset; crimson and violet. But the beach they reached had no changing cabins, no nearby café, and no Mehmet.

Disoriented, due to the deepest human feelings prompted by their rapture, they circled on this unfamiliar beach until Dennis found his trunks and decided they should head East.

Dennis put on his swimming trunks while Myriam slipped back into her bathing suit hoping to arrive back at the beach from which they'd started.

Myriam, skipping as if playing hopscotch, but actually from ecstasy, kept up with Dennis's lengthy strides. Eventually, with darkness all around, they found Mehmet armed with a necessary flashlight. He'd been searching for them next to the changing cabins. He complained: "People thought you'd drowned. You went completely out of sight. And now the changing cabins have closed for the night. You're stuck with wearing wet suits."

Dennis laughed his way out of that one. "You have to be the kindest bridegroom that ever was! Going to be married tomorrow, and worrying about our clothes."

"I'm worrying about my marital bed. I do not want to lie in wet sheets before I wet them. I will lend you pajamas. Ili can produce a nightgown for Myriam."

"Oh? You think I'll need a nightgown?" Myriam's giggles joined in with Dennis's hearty laughter. More liberated every hour, Myriam squeezed a comment between giggles: "I won't be needing one. Though I could use one of her black abayas so we can go see Alexandria's night life."

"Too late to see Ili. I, for one, must not see her now until the marriage ceremony. You may find her at the apartment and borrow her abaya. She may be readying the apartment for our reception tomorrow. Please tell her not to worry about you two staying on after the party. By then, you must have found an apartment of your own."

Mehmet's Islamic code of hospitality had run its course.

Dennis stopped laughing. He sat down at one of the cafe's terrace tables and picked out a newspaper printed in English. He circled the ads of two low-priced apartments.

He asked: "Mehmet, do you have time to help us look at these two?"

"Tonight? All the time in the world. We Muslims do not give each other bachelor parties." Mehmet brought out a pen and circled two different ads. "After we lend you some dry clothes, we can go see these. Cheaper."

A waiter brought two demitasses to the two men. There was no coffee offered to Myriam. She had drawn complaints, seated in her immodest wet bathing suit. It could have passed inspection during daytime when she emerged from a cabin to go straight to the water's edge. It was unacceptable after sunset, in Alexandria an insult to the devout.

Dennis said nothing. Instead, he wondered —bemused—what the waiter might have done if he'd known that Myriam had made love in the nude with nothing but sea water to cover her body.

Mehmet acted as if she was not part of his party.

He continued, speaking to Dennis: "They are directly on the way to one of Alexandria's least beloved sights: King Farouk's summer palace."

Dennis played along, uneasy about drawing farther attention. "Mehmet, why 'least beloved sights?'"

"Because Farouk was not loved. He did not give to the poor. He did not observe the Prophet's orders to help his fellow creatures. He loved his British polo ponies more than his Egyptian subjects. We were glad when he was taken into exile by a British destroyer."

Mehmet called over the waiter and paid his bill. Neither Dennis nor Mehmet had drunk the coffee.

They crossed nearby roads quickly, with Myriam trailing behind, to reach Mehmet's apartment.

There, in the privacy of the bedroom, Dennis tenderly welcomed Myriam back into his arms, and they kissed away any embarrassment caused by the waiter's refusal to serve Myriam.

Back enjoying her new liberation, Myriam laughingly found a brown abaya belonging to Ili, put it on with a shrug, and --while laughter turned to giggles when Dennis tried to fit into one of Mehmet's djellabas—they both knew and accepted that the necessary move to another apartment meant adopting Islamic rules.

Outside, Mehmet stopped a passing bus that had a sign in English for tourists: FAROUK PALACE.

Inside the bus, Mehmet and Dennis had been sandwiched between two women in abayas who were carrying live chickens for sale in tomorrow's plaza market. Each woman carried two chickens upside down, their terrified shrieks obliterating conversation, but not Myriam's giggles. Mehmet managed to growl: "Damn Farouk!"

Myriam's laughter faded. She asked: "Why didn't you like King Farouk? You, personally?"

"All he'd wanted to do was party. Alexandria's night life has not been the same after he left and after the British war time regiments left. Myriam, you would have been disappointed if I tried to show you any night life. We are a city of devout Muslims. The night life is rubbish. And even the palace has been let to get rundown. Look, you can begin to see its gardens: full of weeds and the grass uncut."

Admission to the palace was hours long past. Mehmet told them they hadn't missed anything important. Not far distant there was a crowd pushing and shoving towards a garishly painted apartment complex.

The apartment for lease was being besieged by a queue of anxious would—be renters. Mehmet shouldered himself to the front, disregarding the harassing insults that followed. "I am a bridegroom, being married tomorrow," He shouted in his native language. To Dennis, he murmured in English: "Let me do all the talking. Prices go up when Egyptians believe an American is involved."

"Easy, as I don't speak Arabic. Or, I guess I didn't watch enough movies in Arabic. Ili told Myriam she learned to say 'Hi' and 'So long' for 'Hello' and 'Goodbye' from Hollywood movies.."

"Interesting, because I also learned to speak English mostly from Hollywood movies. But that's not all I learned. Far more important to my life: I learned to lie."

"Lie?"...

"Yes, lie. Myrna Loy's movies were the best for that. I practiced what she preached: 'never tell the truth when a lie works better.' Watch me now, how I handle your rental." Mehmet turned to the owner of the apartment. He didn't speak to him. Instead he emptied his pockets to prove he had no money. After shaking out breadcrumbs and hemp bits, he finally opened his lips to speak. But Dennis tried to interrupt.

"Wait!"

"No, never wait. Just go for what you need." He went back to Arabic. He struck a sorrowful pose for the apartment's owner. "Sir, you have a beautiful apartment. I have nowhere to spend my wedding night. Please Allah by giving me its keys. I will certainly pay you the first months' rent, and the remainder as soon as I get a job."

Whispering for Dennis's benefit, Myriam translated both Mehmet's big lie and the owner's acceptance of it.

The owner bobbed his head like a marionette in a puppet show: "A bridegroom without a bed! This must not be. Surely, Allah the Merciful, prizes those who are generous. You may have the keys."

Myriam had to ante up the rent money because neither Mehmet nor Dennis had enough cash from their waiter jobs..

The disappointed members of the original queue melted away after congratulating Mehmet on his forthcoming marriage. "Allah be praised," one elderly man repeated several times.

A younger man added: "And we must thank his Prophet Mohammed for teaching us to be generous."

On their return bus ride, Mehmet smirked. He said privately to Dennis: "I always get my way. Remember, when it looks like I'll be robbed of my objective, I just lie."

Early on his wedding day, Mehmet left the sofa on which he'd been sleeping, to hurry out to buy fresh fish and cakes for his contribution to the after-ceremony feast.

Myriam accompanied him as far as to a major department store, where she bought two dresses for herself—one to wear for job interviews and the other for the wedding party—and a new abaya for Ili, appropriate for a married woman.

Although they proved almost too heavy for her slight arms to carry, Myriam purchased a pair of embroidered sheets suitable for a wedding night, with embroidered pillowcases for the two cushions that she had missed when Dennis made love.

For her double-bed in their own apartment, Myriam bought bottom sheets only as she knew that top sheets would never be used.

Mehmet returned only minutes before the marriage ceremony was scheduled. There was no ice box in his kitchenette: he placed the cooked fishes and the cakes on his sparse buffet, then hurried to shave and shower.

Ili's parents and grandparents arrived before the guests. Ili's mother—who was perfectly familiar with the apartment because she hadn't given permission for the marriage until after

Mehmet said it had been bought and paid for—proceeded to brew a large amount of mint tea. She had brought with her a selection of tea pots and placed them like marching soldiers on a table alongside the boiling pot.

Ili arrived late. After waiting six years for this day, Ili suffered an embarrassing delay in finding a taxi that would stop for an unaccompanied Muslim female.

As she entered the apartment a hush came from her gabbing relations. They were astonished that Ili had transformed herself into what appeared to be a slim, gorgeous, young woman. Her scarf hed hear neck. Her ankle-length dress hid her fat legs. A massive head-dress hid her thinning hair.

Her bra masked sunken breast and a very tight corset had played its parts.

The stream of guests knew nothing of her efforts to improve herself. Only her immediate relatives had seen her previously without an abaya and head covering.

Mehmet, absolutely delighted with her appearance, whispered to Dennis: "Now you can believe why I waited so long for Ili. She looked like this when her grandmother first invited me to see her with the object of having her as my fiancée."

"Very attractive," Dennis said. He was amazed at the change but could not remark on it because he shouldn't have been able to see her face although he'd slept in what was basically her apartment.

Myriam hurried to wrap arms around Ili's hidden waist. "A little wedding gift," she breathed, handing a bottle of Chanel Number Five to Ili. "Wear it in bed, and nothing else. That's what Chanel does."

Ili didn't giggle. She maintained a very serious expression, as if not yet sure about getting married.

Her paternal grandfather began the traditional Nikah ceremony by reading a passage from the Koran and then extending a copy of the Koran toward Ili. Next, he pointed at Mehmet and inquired: "Do you accept this man for your husband?"

Iliana nodded. There was a pause, before Mehmet's father asked a similar question of Mehmet, substituting the word "wife:"

He nodded, and unexpectedly added: "I want to make her happy."

Ili's father, very much a traditionalist, frowned at this interruption. "I am a witness. My son Mohammed is a witness. Give us the certificate to sign. Ili, you sign. Mehmet, have you given her the deed to this apartment? If so, you sign."

Playfully, Mehmet pretended he could not find the deed. He held up the apartment's two keys. "Will these do?"

Both father and grandfather turned angry. "This is not a serious way to behave. The deed, Mehmet!"

Mehmet's face turned grey. His attempt to lighten the festivity had turned extremely flat. "I have the deed. Look! Here it is!" Not satisfied with his means of escape, he added—very aware that it was a lie—hand on heart, "All paid for. No mortgage.'"

Solemnly Ili's grandfather grasped the official-looking paper and read it aloud as if he'd never seen it before;"Bring the marriage contract." he summoned Mehmet's father, his hands shaking.

The grandfather, father, and two witnesses signed. Ili, still flustered from the rude interruption to her marriage ceremony, signed. Mehmet signed.

Ili's grandmother brought out two teapots and started filling cups. Her mother carved up the fish wellingtons and served them.

There was no kiss between bride and groom. No rings were exchanged. But their smiles had returned.

A cousin had brought a wind-up Victrola and placed a record with music simulating a muezzin's cry to prayer. Several of the elderly men went to their knees thinking it must be time for prayers.

Mehmet and Iliana danced together, shocking the older ladies, who all wore head scarves as if they were on a public street.

A late guest brought about a shout from Mehmet. Dennis followed that with a huge roar. "Ahmed!"

His former bunks mate had arrived from his faked sick bed in Cairo.

"What, you rascal, you aren't dead?" Mehmet joked, relieved that a newcomer was unaware of the drama of a few minutes earlier.

In English, for Dennis's benefit, Ahmed yelled: "Fine! I'm fine. Sick leave over. I'll be flying with you to Tobruk to join the 'DEVERON.'"

Ahmed had brought his wife, Fila, a very liberated Muslim.

Instead of hanging back in this room of strangers, Fila sidled across the floor, purposely bumping her hip against one of the younger good-looking men.

He spilled the mint tea from his cup. This man was not an easy mark .He was wearing a traditional djellaba and slippers. He glared at Fila, muttering: "I am a devout Muslim. Here in Alexandria we do not play the games of Cairo's women."

Thinking she was seeing another sympathizer of female modernity in Islam, Myriam failed to dig for more indications of Fila's real character and joined her at the buffet. Smiling warmly, she suggested: "I've hidden a bottle of whiskey in the kitchenette. Want some?"

"I like men, not women," Fila shot her return. "I can get all the whiskey I want in Cairo. It's the men who prove scarce but not so scarce that I'd go anywhere private with a woman."

She bumped a thigh against a second man. This one was wearing a western-style suit, not a djellaba.

He proved accessible. Steering Fila to the empty corridor outside, he led her to a taxi on the road beyond.

Ahmed watched them with a resigned scowl He said: "I had a test for TB. Clear, Allah be praised. I'd worried so much I could pass TB to Fila. I'm always thinking of her. You'd think I'd be enough for her when I'm home. But no, she's always looking for a better man. I must have picked up something else bad when we were in port in Barcelona. Fila has it now. I pity the men she picks up."

Myriam, shocked for once, left the three men and returned to Ili.

The bride was sipping pensively from her teacup. She said: "I have never felt that Ahmed was a suitable friend for Mehmet. Not devout at all."

Myriam changed the subject. "Ili, did you ever have trouble keeping men away during those long six years of being Mehmet's fiancée?"

"I met very few men, after I'd become engaged. Once my grandmother did bring to our home a possible substitute, who had money enough to get married right away. He did try to touch me inappropriately. I believe he wanted to test if I'd prove frigid. I have a girl cousin who deals with that sort of thing in her own way: she's a heavy smoker, and she just burns any fresh men with a cigarette. My method is different. I said to this man: 'You are so gallant. And I heard you are a most devout Muslim. I feel certain I have misunderstood what just happened.'"

"And?"

"He stood up and got out of the house. Try my method, if ever you have need."

Ahmed had gone in search of the whiskey, and Ili had followed him although still sipping her tea.

Myriam rejoined Mehmet and Dennis. She said: "I'm learning that Ili has some special facets."

"Yes, my Ili—my wife! She was so brave during the approach towards Alexandria of General Rommel's Nazi army. Rommel's forces came within a few miles of Alexandria. Many of our women were evacuated. Ili stayed."

Discreetly whispering, Myriam suggested: "Shall we prompt your guests to leave? We can make a big thing of packing up."

"Yes, please. I hate those forever wedding parties that go on and on, when the bridegroom is eager to get into bed with his wife."

A Muezzin's call to prayer echoed from a nearby Mosque, which caused all the men to go to their knees and face Mecca. When they stood again, Myriam was in the apartment's doorway carrying the sheets she'd bought earlier.

That hint was good enough. Dennis's loud: "Goodbye," gave the final message. As if The End had come up on a movie screen, all the guests filed out the door. Ili gave a huge wink to her parents and grandfather, who didn't delay.

Dennis thought he'd caught a glint of sensuality in Ili's thirty-year-old eyes.

Out on the street, waiting for the bus labeled FAROUK PALACE, Myriam hugged Dennis, and said: "I hope they find wonder in their bed. We certainly did."

In the next week their semi-furnished apartment remained barely livable while Dennis and Myriam looked for paying jobs. Myriam, although tutored at home and with no college degree, had the advantage that she spoke three languages. She landed a low salaried position at Barclay's Bank.

Dennis was offered nothing.

On the Friday, when all Muslim Alexandria shut down while its devout citizens attended their mosques, he found that the United States consulate was open for business and prepared to discuss the addition of Myriam's married name to his passport.

At the consulate he was shown into the private office of a Vice Consul named Silvester Gregory, a pompous pimpled Yale graduate.

The Vice-Consul's first query centered around the validity of the DEVERON wedding. "Have you received a certificate from the Bermuda Marriage Bureau?"

"Not yet. But I telephoned my branch of the National City Bank in New York and was assured that the necessary $265 had been paid out."

"We can't re-issue you a passport with the addition of Myriam McLeary until you can show that certificate." Having used the royal "We," Silvester Gregory now tapped the crystal face of his watch, stood up from his desk, and announced: "I am invited to lunch by the British Consul General. Come back when you have that receipt."

Dismissed like a naughty schoolboy, Dennis found that he had nothing else important to do until five o'clock when Myriam would leave for home from her Barclays Bank job.

A group of tourists were urged by their guide to mount their private bus. Dennis joined them in the role of an escort, without having to pay. A local woman, wearing a headscarf twisted around her neck and the brown dress of an unmarried girl, presided with a microphone describing each landmark in three languages: passable English, faulty German, and terrible unaccented French,

She stood hunched up next to a brawny driver who spoke English with a Serbian accent. A refugee, he'd come as a 'displaced person' to Cairo after the Nazis over-ran Yugoslavia, and he stayed on. He was totally unfamiliar with the streets and sights and twice missed a road and a landmark.

The female guide, whose light mustache became more apparent when she struggled with the tourists' three languages, grew upset each time. "I'll lose my job if you mess up again," she complained.

"Do you carry water on this bus?" An Englishwoman inquired politely.

"You are supposed to bring your own," the guide growled in as dark a tone as the color of her mustache. "Ladies and gentlemen, we are approaching what remains of Alexandria's world famous libraries. These ruins once contained at least ten percent of all of the world's wisdom: they were once the Temple of Serapis, which survived the fire that consumed the major grand library near the harbor. It is believed that Julius Caesar, cut off by an Egyptian fleet when he was pursuing Pompey, ordered the harbor's ships burned which ignited the library and the Temple."

The Englishwoman, again—very politely—but determined, posed a question: "Who was Pompey? Of course, I know about Julius Caesar…"

This time her guide ignored the question and veered into the salacious history of Cleopatra's loves. "Did you know that Caesar's only beloved son was the one he had by Cleopatra. She had three other children by Mark Anthony: a twin boy and girl, and a third son."

A German tourist sang out: "I know she had herself hidden in a rug to be presented to Caesar past his guards…"

The guide jumped to another subject. "We cannot end today's tour to Alexandria's museum, because it is closed for our Holy Day. You will miss incredible artefacts said to be retained from when Alexander of Macedonia took the city. Sorry, but you are all invited to the Grand Hotel for coffee to make up for that. And remember, I have a box here for any of you kind visitors who wish to give me a tip."

Dennis glided out of the private bus and found one that had the sign FAROUK'S PALACE.

At home, he found Myriam, naked, emerging from their tiny bathroom's shower, her face wet from tears not the shower.

"My darling. What's happened?"

"After work I went to the nearest mosque."

"Yes. I'm fine with that. I'm beginning to admire the Muslims. But, at the Mosque, what—"

Myriam found her old brown dress and struggled into it. For a few seconds, she could not speak: she was sobbing, gasping. Finally she howled: "They cut off her head. Beheaded her!" Then bleating like a horribly beaten child, she added: "They killed Auntie. They cut off, off, off her head."

"Who? Which Auntie? Where?"

"You must remember the frail old lady who accompanied me to the Grand Emporium? In Kusadasi! She was the one who left the store wearing my burqa so I could escape to marry you."

"The lady who had Parkinson's? Walked with such small wavering steps?"

"That one, yes. She wanted to go home to Saudi Arabia for treatment. My father's aunt. My great-aunt, who hated the way women have to live in Saudi Arabia. She taught me to want to be liberated."

"Beheaded? You sure? Who told you?"

"I was told by a woman who met us at Ili's wedding. Of the Old School. "She warned me, Your husband will be next." She knows where we live and we gave her our address at the wedding party."

"Darling, we'll leave here right away. What do you think: try Cairo? Mix in with the big crowds there?"

"Cairo, for the moment. We'll catch a bus. Can I cram my new dresses into your duffle bag?"

Bent with an elderly person's faltering steps, the tears constantly streaming like a broken faucet, Myriam dealt with her dresses, and carefully added a frying pan to the duffle bag. "We'll have to find another apartment. I'll cook. We can't eat out, for fear of being seen. We can't go to a hotel: hotels ask for passports. Don't forget yours."

Dennis patted the passport that was still in his jacket pocket. He regretted sorely that he hadn't been able to add Myriam's name. He knew they shouldn't leave Egypt while she still had to use her Saudi passport. When Dennis had been in prison, he'd heard sorry stories of the difficulty of crossing a border without a passport stamped with a visa.

They caught the last bus leaving Alexandria.

Chapter 5

Cairo, Egypt

Oh, Cairo! How many generations and how many heroes have passed your way: Alexander of Macedonia, Julius Caesar, Mark Antony, Napoleon Bonaparte, Emperor Haile Selassie, Winston Churchill. Always the same rich soil when the Nile overflows, always the plagues of locusts and sandstorms, always phenomenally rich foreigners and very poor fellahin Egyptians. Always with crowds too thick and churches too empty. Its smell of thousands perspiring in contrast to a courtesane's Chanel perfume wafting from the terrace of Shepherd's Hotel. Millionaire shooting birds from boats in the Nile. Dead dog's carcasses rolling in canals.

Cairo for Dennis and Myriam was a magnet for increasingly great love-making.

Cairo's huge streetcar terminal was situated on Atabel al-Khadra Square. Dennis, loaded with his duffle bag, groggy with worry and lack of sleep, bought a copy of Cairo's second oldest newspaper: The Al-Ahram. He couldn't read it: Myriam needed to translate the section that featured Apartments For Rent.

"We can't afford any of them."

"You can. My money stopped when Auntie's head was cut off. She'd been financing my escape. But I learned a few good tips while I worked at Barclay's Bank: in twenty-four hours your Deedee Murray can wire you enough for a month's rental. More, if necessary." Myriam, comfortable in English and in the Arabic language, scanned the paper and selected two one-roomers in quiet neighborhoods.

By the time the Muezzins had made their second calls for prayers, Dennis was negotiating the price for a short lease on the second bedroom-with-bath they viewed. It was adequate.

The furnishings proved awful. Kitchen repairs and a plumber for the overflowing toilet made the cheap price not so cheap.

Myriam laughed off these niggling troubles by using her Alexandria-bought bottom sheet to ready their bed. Within seconds she was on it, stripping naked.

"I love this room," Dennis joined in her laughter until deep throat kisses drowned it. Myriam interrupted them.

"Do you think I'll get pregnant?" she asked Dennis.

During the passing weeks, Myriam asked that same question two or three times a day. She'd felt an enormous desire to be pregnant.

She'd remained safely in their St. Mark's quarter.

Dennis had secured a half-day job in an American Company with hopes there existed a ladder to get a higher salary eventually. Not easy, he still had little knowledge of Arabic.

The job paid for their groceries.

Dennis did all of the shopping, which included medicines for a heavy cold that had hit Myriam.

Myriam hated having a cold. She wanted her malaise to be caused by a more hopeful outcome. "Not pregnant, still. Just sick from this stupid cold. Have you ever heard of a woman hoping for morning sickness? I do. But still, no sign of pregnancy yet. Dennis, do you think I could dare go to a mosque, and pray?"

"Not unless you mind risking being beheaded. I think that mosques will be among the first places your father will have searched. After all, it was at a mosque where you walked into that woman from the wedding party. You might try a church

119

instead. Or go see the pyramids and the sphinx. Visit Egypt's greatest museums. I doubt those would appeal to people from Saudi Arabia. See a Special Church. Coptic, for instance."

"If that's what you want," she said.

"Yes to a church. And we live in the Hanging Church's quarter: I can take a bus. I can sneak in a side door or go in the back way. Quietly. You can buy American clothes for me and I'll do my hair in one of those new ponytails. No one will think of me as from Saudi Arabia."

"If that's what you want. I'm not one to try to make you turn your back on the Muslim faith."

"After Islamic law permitted cutting off my old Auntie's head, I'm ready to change. To become a Christian. I like that they were told to forget all the old laws of the prophets, to only love God above all, and neighbors as themselves…"

Myriam, leaving the apartment, studied the surroundings she hadn't permitted herself to notice earlier. The neighborhood, very old, dating—who knew—to Roman times, lacked sanitation. There were human feces and urine every few steps. She hurried to the nearest bus stop and hailed a post-war vehicle that advertised its destination in English as The Hanging Church.

On board, she paid the fare and carefully sat between two elderly women covered in abayas.

Myriam had read about The Hanging Church. She knew it was dedicated to St. Mary, and had sections dating back to the Fifth Century. The oldest part was suspended on the ruins of a Roman tower and been used for many purposes during its long history: as a political base, and as a Patriarch's palace, in addition to being a place of worship. It survived the arrival of Muslim conquerors in the Eighth Century, according to legend because a priest revived the story in Mathew about moving a mountain.

Myriam scurried up the wide white stairway leading to the tall narrow front door and slid into its interior into what she hoped was in a secure out-of-the-way location.

Her view of the nave was uninterrupted: she saw its multiple crystal chandeliers lighting the icons and ancient murals. Two murals caught her special attention: one of Jesus receiving black visitors from Ethiopia, the other of a sleeping St. Joseph protected by a heavily winged angel. She wondered: Did either event actually happen?

She was staring at the wooden roof, made in an upside down version of Noah's ark, when a rude woman pinched her arm.

Fila! The woman was Ahmed's wild wife, who had left Mehmet and Ili's wedding reception with a man other than her husband. In Arabic, she snarled: "What you doing here? Why in a church: when you are a Muslim?"

"I'm a tourist, visiting the city's landmarks. But, you? This is your city. You can't say you are a tourist." Myriam shoved Fila behind the church's elaborate wooden screen.

"I will tell on you to the religious police, if you dare to say you saw me here."

"But the police will say you must have been in the church yourself to have seen me here." Myriam toyed with Fila, who was far outclassed by her in the intelligence stakes.

Fila had no chance to reply, because a blond Swedish sailor sneaked up behind her and grabbed one of her breasts while with the other hand he playfully touched one of Myriam's. "Nothing I like better than a threesome," he chortled.

In his broken, poor use of Arabic, he tormented Myriam further by what was nearly a shout: "I'd like a carrot-head better than that fake blonde Fila. Let's find a hotel."

Myriam broke away and managed to locate a flight of stairs. But he was quicker and reached the top simultaneously. She opened a door to find herself on a long balcony overlooking the street.

He grabbed her again.

Unmeaning, Myriam's struggles were sending one of his eager legs closer to her most private part. She tried to bite the man and was uselessly snapping her teeth in air when a priest appeared on the balcony.

Heavily bearded, wearing a black cassock topped by an oversized Coptic cross on its long chain, the priest did not chastise the sailor. He kicked him, and slapped him in the face. "Get out, you heathen. Go back to your immoral country."

With an amazing push, that almost sent the sailor from the balcony to the street below, he propelled the sailor back to the inside stairs to rid his church of the human trash that had invaded it.

To Myriam, he said gently: "I see you are wearing what the westerners call a wedding ring. That man could have caused you to commit adultery. Go home to your husband."

Plagued by a series of shakes that interrupted her stance every few moments like a dying flickering light bulb, Myriam eventually eased down the church stairs and found her way past its entrance and back to the bus stop.

Myriam was still shaking when she returned to their bedroom-with-bath. Hurtling into Dennis's arms, she cried: "We've got to leave here. Fila, Ahmed Rashid's wife, has seen me. She might find a way to let the Saudi Consul know I am in Cairo without implicating herself. Where can we go?"

"We'll go somewhere because sounds like we have to go. We'll find a place for us."

Chapter 6

May, 1948 Jerusalem

On May 18, 1948 in Eretz, David Ben-Gurion, head of the Jewish Agency, proclaimed the establishment of the State of Israel. That same day, the President of the friendly USA, Harry Truman, recognized the new nation.

On May 19, Dennis and Myriam crossed Israel's border with Egypt at Taba Borda. From there they proceeded as necessary to find a train.

They took a train which had been run formerly by the British, when Palestine was under British Mandate.

"Look, Dennis! That's where Lawrence of Arabia was captured by the Ottoman troops when this land was part of Turkey. See? There's a sign."

"Your eyes are so much better than mine. I can see the sign, but I sure can't read it."

Lately, Dennis had realized that Myriam surpassed him intellectually and in other ways, but he welcomed that. Not disparaging the sexual bond which had entranced them both, he reveled in her knowledge of other subjects. The fact, that she spoke Arabic and he did not, could have somewhat diminished their love. That had not happened. Now her fascination with local history did bruise him.

She'd added: "Poor Lawrence of Arabia, he accomplished so much but was sodomized by those troops worse than a kid in a male brothel."

Dennis said nothing. He ground his teeth and pinched his thumbs with his forefingers.

When their train finally edged into the stifling-hot Jerusalem station, he lifted down his duffle bag from its overhead shelf feeling grateful to carry a different kind of heavy load.

As in Cairo, he bought a local newspaper and Myriam perused the ads for one room apartments. She murmured: "Maybe I should look for one-rooms, not an apartment? Who knows if we can get jobs to pay for an apartment?"

Myriam was proven right. Jobs were nearly non-existent because many intellectuals and scientists were pouring into Jerusalem from countries as far away as Australia. Less trained minds were flooding into Israel to take the lower positions.

Depressed after weeks of no success for either of them, Dennis had to periodically ask for funds overseen for release by Deedee in New York. He'd spent what had been earned as interest, now he'd hit on his $10,000 capital. He'd reached the $9,000 level.

To distract himself from financial worries Dennis visited the Church of the Holy Sepulcher. He visited the cave said to be the place where Jesus Christ had been lain after he was crucified. He saw—dulled-by-age—white cloths that could have been Jesus's shroud. A deep sensation overpowered Dennis. He had to leave the church: he was shaking badly, although he desperately wanted to sing. Sing? Sing!

He left the old city and stopped a bus lettered for his own quarter. He rushed home to hug and kiss Myriam. He did not tell her about the experience in the church.

When she wanted to visit the Coptic Church and its monastery, he strongly advised her to choose between the Citadel and the Jews' Wailing Wall. "The Citadel, or if you prefer—The Tower of David—is near the Jaffa Gate entrance on the western edge of the old city. It dates from the Ottoman and Mamluk days. You'd find that interesting enough. You might get the creeps at the Wailing Wall, although I hear it's rather fun to watch some of the visitors slipping notes between its stones."

Myriam argued: "I want to see where Emperor Haile Selassie sent his wife to live during the cold winters he spent in London. He endured those winters waiting for a battle that would end World War II that would release his country from being held by the AXIS. She lived here in the Coptic Monastery. I'm sure I read an interesting magazine article about that somewhere."

"Maybe the Empress stayed in the nunnery! I don't think the Coptic monks will ever let you get near either of those two places. Honestly, go see the Wailing Wall."

"I've been saving that to take my mother there."

"Your mother!"

"Yes. I've been corresponding with Mommy for weeks…"

Sternly, in the base tone he only used for naughty children, Dennis coughed out: "I haven't seen any letters."

"I'm not stupid, dear. I sent them by hand with a girl who works in the bathing suit shop where I've been offered a job after Ramadan. Remember the shop? The girl's from Kusadasi, and she goes home there on weekends to be with her family. She's been my very own private courier."

"Has your mother settled on a date?"

"Yes. She arrives in two weeks. She's staying over-night. Has to return to her sick sister."

"Over-night! But we have only this one room."

"She wouldn't think of sleeping here. She knows better than to draw Saudi killers to me. She had to save herself from killers when she was first divorced. We'll only meet on Tourists' buses."

"Not safe."

"Please don't worry. My mother's often taken for an Englishwoman. We'll take a tour for English people."

Two weeks later, on the carefully chosen bus, Myriam almost gave the game away when she saw her mother again after those many lonely months.

She shrieked: "Mommy! My beautiful Mommy."

And her mother dropped her façade of tourist to rush to take Myriam into her arms.

Conversation was nearly impossible with the Tour Guide bellowing into a microphone, translating her description of the sites the bus passed. But mother and daughter were entranced beyond caring what she said. It was enough to whisper half phrases between hugs and kisses.

Eventually their bus came to the huge plaza leading to the Wailing Wall. Most passengers disembarked from this private tour bus, but one woman cringed in her seat. She moaned, "I should never have come. There's going to be a blood bath someday. It could be today. The Palestinians know where to target the most vulnerable, unarmed Jews."

"What about us?" Myriam, almost playfully asked: "Darling, precious, wonderful Mommy; should we be cowards, and stay in these seats?"

"Of course not. Dearest child, didn't I teach you to always go forward? Get what you want? I didn't complain when you eloped with a ship's waiter! I believed in your destiny."

Myriam helped her mother handle the bus's high steps leading to the ground: it seared her heart to see how much her mother's health had deteriorated.

Limping, pushing forward, her mother continued to hold firmly to Myriam's left arm. Sticking close to the British tourists, they did not check out the foreigners of varied nationalities swirling behind the praying Jews.

That day the other tourists included many Germans, some Americans, and a tight-knit group of men from Saudi Arabia, distinctive in their collared djellabas and the checkered table-cloth-like cotton squares topped by circular hoops they wore on their heads.

When Myriam and her mother had completed the tour, Mommy said:"Come with me to my Hotel. We have just enough time for tea before I have to catch my train."

Gloriously happy to have more precious minutes with Mommy, Myriam 's delight prodded her to agree although she felt through intuition that this was an invitation as dangerous as a chocolate candy with an arsenic center.

But the sad moment arrived soon after tea-time when she helped Mommy with the difficult locks on her overnight case. Myriam followed the porter carrying it while Mommy paid her bill at the Cashier.

Myriam sensed how much Mommy was suffering as they reached the taxi rank. Her hands fluttering like moths about to be burned by fire, Mommy wrapped herself around her daughter. Both women couldn't stop weeping.

When Mommy gave her order to the cab driver: "Railroad Station...Please." the moment became so terrible for Myriam that she attempted to thrust herself inside the taxi. "No, Precious Child, you chose your destiny and I must now pray to Allah that you will be happy." She closed the door.

Emotionally strained, Myriam weaved toward a distant bus stop. Her handkerchief, now useless, was drenched with tears. She threw it into the gutter.

At the same moment two Saudi Arabian thugs pounced on Myriam, covered her in a brown abaya, and pushed her into a waiting sedan that had its windows blackened. One brown hand smothered her screams until a tanned hand slapped adhesive over her mouth.

The two men threw her on the floor. She felt a terrible revulsion. Was she going to be raped?

No.

They managed to roll her into a rug. In this rug they moved her to a private airplane in which she was flown to Riyadh, Saudi Arabia.

Still in the rug, Myriam was lifted into yet another limousine.

One more heave, and she found herself inside the lobby of her father's imposing mansion.

Breathing frantically for some air, she was helped to her stiffened knees by a heavy

BEATRICE FAIRBANKS CAYZER

woman who had the cruel face of a prison warden.

While being professionally chained, Myriam looked past the woman to see her father enter the lobby.

He stared at her stomach.

Snarling with the pent-up hatred of a kenneled wolfhound, he spat out: "Are you pregnant?"

Myriam, her mouth still taped, couldn't speak.

She shook her head, although feeling another nail had just hammered her to a cross.

"Negative."

"Wicked daughter! You have disgraced our family name. Disgraced me. But I will not be denied the founding of my dynasty. For all that you ran away with a waiter to lose your purity believing in a contemptable shipboard farce, I will provide a proper Muslim husband for you. There are some decent men for sale.

Money still reigns in Saudi Arabia. But first I will break that rebellious spirit of yours. And if you turn out to be pregnant, I'll send an abortionist to get rid of any baby. It's out to the desert with you."

Her father cracked his knuckles. Two fierce-faced women appeared, wearing brown abayas…The women could have found a place in a zoo specializing in cannibal-like animals. A jackal would have run away in terror from those two Saudi women.

One produced ordinary police-use handcuffs and clicked them on to Myriam's wrists. The second shoved her into an ordinary wheel-chair, to which she was secured by more chains around her waist and feet to be secured by strong locks. Her father didn't watch. With a shrug; he left the lounge. She didn't have to guess, but she didn't have to grab what destination was because she knew what it was. Best because she knew.

The first woman tore off the strip of adhesive.

In Arabic, Myriam pleaded: "I must use a bathroom."

The second woman trundled Myriam to a garage, where the chains were temporarily released while Myriam was permitted to use the servants' toilet. That job done, the chains were replaced, the locks clicked, and Myriam's wheel-chair gave way to a back seat in a truck driven by a large black man.

The two scary women had to share the back seat next to Myriam. The heat caused all three to perspire like the Amazon jungle's wild boars.

Riyadh's hellish temperature had not dissipated with the arrival of night.

Leaving Riyadh, there were fewer lights gleaming in houses, but Myriam could see families congregating on their roofs to catch a breath of air.

At least she could get air through both nostrils and her mouth now, and she'd escaped the total darkness within the asphyxiating rug.

Myriam wondered how Cleopatra had survived her trip to Caesar's side.

Without being able to look at her watch, Myriam was unable to judge the distance covered, but she knew her destination. Her father's mother had inherited an old-time desert home that came with her dowry.

During her annual six months of forced sojourns as a captive of her father, Myriam had heard that it was a horror, only used to chastise wicked female family members.

Myriam had learned that one cousin had died in the house, when its skeletal staff of cook and housekeeper had quit their jobs and left her without food or water.

Dawn was breaking, with no cheerful sunrise due to a rainstorm, when the truck finally arrived at "Granny's house." It had no driveway or garden. It had no lights.

Inside, Myriam was eventually unshackled from the handcuffs only to be thrust into a very bare room. Its one door and tiny window were promptly secured by heavy locks. Within minutes Myriam heard the truck leave, with its black driver, and the two sadistic women wardens aboard.

Next to her bedroom there was no toilet, no shower. There were many cushions strewn in a corner to sleep on, strips of cloth for toilet use, and three bowls. The largest, sparsely filled, contained water with which to clean herself, the second was for drinking, the third for urine and feces.

Left alone, Myriam—to keep her sanity— forced herself to mentally replay over and over the happy days of her honeymoon and months in Egypt.

Chapter 7

Tel Aviv, Israel; Bombay and Digboi, India

Coincidentally the receipt from Bermuda, giving official notice that Dennis had paid for his marriage certificate, arrived on the same day that Myriam's Mommy traveled from Turkey.

Outfitted in her old brown un-married girl's dress to show Mommy that she cared about the last months they had spent together, Myriam had left home early for the Tourist Bus Agency, where they'd agreed to meet.

Dennis went to the inter-city bus station that offered transport to central Tel Aviv.

"What a beautiful city," he said under his breath as the bus reached its destination. He was very pleased to be back in a town that had buildings overlooking a beach. Dennis determined to have a swim before he left to return to Jerusalem.

He had a bit of luck when he entered the U.S. Consulate. Dennis learned that he was being referred to an assistant. The assistant proved to be both kind and efficient. His new passport, paid for and nestling in his pocket like a friendly canary had included Myriam's name and photograph for all officialdom to see.

Following his earlier plan for a swim, Dennis headed for the nearest beach that offered changing rooms. He decided against buying swimming trunks, judging he could rush to the shoreline in his blue briefs without breaking any laws.

"Dennis, over here. Let's have coffee together," A familiar voice stopped him from entering a changing room. "I'm Mehmet! Don't you care about your old friends?" Mehmet was seated alone at a table for two on the promenade above the beach.

Dennis, his shoes filled with beach residue, was slow to gain the promenade. He knew he couldn't try to avoid Mehmet: not after all he did to help Myriam get on the DEVERON, and having attended his wedding and lived in his apartment: "Hello, Mehmet. How goes it? Iliana pregnant yet?"

Mehmet's welcoming smile waned. "No, no baby on the horizon, but it has been okay trying." He brightened: "I called you over because I've got tremendous news regarding a job. I learned how in Digboi, India the oil people are paying $32 a day for unskilled folks who know nothing about drilling for oil. Interested?" Mehmet was gloating like a chef who has pulled a perfect cake from his oven.

Dennis sat down and took the menu to scan its prices. He ordered two coffees from a hovering waiter, and frowned as he turned to Mehmet. He knew the unlovely side of Mehmet's money-hungry character: his propensity to show off and to exaggerate. "You sure about that? The $32 a day?"

Mehmet's left hand went to his jacket pocket and drew out an official looking paper: "Here's my contract. A Visa will be provided tomorrow," he added."

This time there was no need to exaggerate. Dennis read the contract, nodded in agreement, and passed it back. "I'm glad for you, Mehmet. When do you leave for India?"

"Tomorrow. I'm hitching a ride on an airplane. Honestly, no fooling. Seems like Ben Gurion was in Geneva recently having a skin problem looked at, and it occurred to him that Israel needed an airline. Don't ask me how those are connected: skin problem and airline. Before you could spell airline, he'd got airplanes, pilots, mechanics and airfields lined up. I'm friends with one of the mechanics. He told me that several experimental flights are planned and he's on the one to Bombay. He'll get me on board. Want to come?'

"I'll have to ask Myriam." The coffees arrived, and the two men stopped talking to compare flavors with what they got in Egypt.

"Coffees better in Alexandria. Why ask Myriam about coming to Digboi? Who wears the pants in your family? Don't tell me you've got to get permission!"

"I love her beyond anything in the world. And anyway, eventually I'll get a decent job in Israel. There are export companies that need English-speaking employees."

"But not paying $32 a day. Here, take this bit of paper and write down the address of the local Digboi Oil Company offices. And make a note of my hotel's telephone number. I've got to get going. I really hope you come to India." Mehmet disappeared in the crowds of vacationers on the promenade. He'd left his half of the bill unpaid.

Dennis settled the bill, shrugged and made his way to the bus station to return to Jerusalem. His idea of going for a swim had been left too late.

At home, their one room was dark. No Myriam.

She hadn't left a supper or a note for him.

Dennis heated yesterday's potatoes and beans, put on his pajama bottoms and went to bed.

He couldn't sleep.

Like the scenes from a Hollywood horror movie, his mind was filled with terror plots: Myriam chloroformed and flown to Saudi Arabia, bound and gagged. Myriam knocked unconscious, and raped. Myriam drowned.

It wasn't a Frankenstein's monster that perpetrated these scenes. it was a Saudi in flowing garments.

After midnight, he left their bed and dressed in his best street clothes to be ready for any Myriam emergency.

Dawn came, no Myriam.

Dennis put his mind to work: who knew Marion here in Jerusalem? After much thought, he recalled the two girls in the bathing suit shop who had offered her a job for after Ramadan. One of those women had delivered letters to Myriam's mother when going home weekends to her Ephesus family.

The shop wouldn't open before nine a.m. Dennis forced himself to eat a croissant and some cereal, aware he needed to strengthen himself for whatever bad news would come.

At nine a.m. precisely he was walking toward the shop when his attention was drawn to yellow tapes many yards away: yellow tapes proclaiming death. Two police cars, an ambulance and a fire truck were parked nearby. A crowd had gathered.

Women in abayas dried their eyes: one spectator vomited.

Recognizing Dennis as an American, one officer slowed his approach, saying in English: "Sir, you don't want to get too close. Blood everywhere. The two women in this shop were beheaded last evening: their heads have rolled like bowling balls. Sorry, if they were your friends. Would you like to speak to the news reporters about your relationship?"

Dennis turned on his heel to return home to the ever-ready duffel bag. Mourning the girls would have to wait. He certainly couldn't appear in a court to weigh in about their good character. Their deaths were the typical signature of Myriam's father: beheading anyone who helped Myriam. He would be next if the Saudi thugs could find him.

Myriam was not on the beheading list because her father had no other option except to rely on this one daughter to beget a dynasty.

Dennis felt sure she was already in Riyadh with her father.

Now Dennis needed money. His New York funds were near depletion: he would need to earn a good salary to finance his own trip to Saudi Arabia to rescue his wife. He dug out the paper with Mehmet's number.

After packing lightly, he headed grimly for the same inter-city bus station.

His bus for Tel Aviv was almost empty. Dennis could rest his duffel bag on the empty seat next to his. He slept well during the ride, and was ready to meet the rest of this tumultuous day by locating Mehmet and be taken to the local offices of the Digboi Oil Company.

Chapter 8

Summer 1948, Saudi Arabia's northern desert

For her first three months in that room Myriam needed all her strength of character to survive. Her three bowls were filled by the servant girl who had no tongue. Conversation was nil. The girl brought her local-style food: flat bread, beans and rice; she dealt with the three bowls, refreshing the water and dispensing with the urine and stools.

Myriam learned more about the two other members of the girl's family who were also employed on the estate. Her father, called Youssef, was a Bedouin former camel jockey, who served as guardian of the house. Myriam knew that he was armed with a rifle because deer were shot occasionally for a change of diet. The girl's mother only acted as cook: she hadn't a clue what a recipe was. Her only menus consisted of rice and beans. After Myriam's arrival, she never came near Myriam. If she passed Myriam's room , she would call on Allah to be kept safe.

It was during the first month of her captivity that Myriam had one joy to help her through this agonizing time: her menses didn't arrive. She was finally pregnant with Dennis's child.

She knew how vital it was to keep that news from getting to her father, who would be quick to order an abortion.

To provide menses color blood to smear on the napkins provided once every month along with her meals, Myriam used her dinner knife to cut the insides of her fingers to coat the napkins appropriately with blood.

The earlier wished-for Morning Sickness was not too severe, but she needed her dinner knife to pry open her window in order to pour out the vomit into scrub outside.

A day came when the mute servant girl gave Myriam two meals at once and extra water bowls. The girl was wearing make-up: mascara and eyeliner, lipstick and rouge. She danced her shoulders to show off a new abaya, that garment used in public. She was leaving the house. For a day, a week, or forever?

Within minutes after delivering the extra food and water, the girl was shouted at by her mother: "Hurry, hurry! Papa has our camels ready. We do not want to miss the first race!"

Were they leaving for the Camel Races' Fair outside Riyadh?

Youssef could be heard preparing two camels for his women.to ride to the Fair. Those two camels, anticipating welcome exercise, bellowed contentedly while Youssef brought them to their knees.

Bu, as for himself, he didn't leave. How long would Youssef remain at the house? Wouldn't a former camel jockey want to go to camel races?

He must have wanted to go. But he was propelled to go out only when a passing truck driver—stopping for water—advised him that both his wife and daughter had been arrested by the Religious Police and were in serious trouble at the Camel Races' Fair.

After the departure of the truck driver, Myriam heard Youssef preparing himself and his best camel to leave "Grandma's estate."

As the day grew longer, Myriam knew that she'd been left alone in the house without any more food or water.

She wondered: how many days would it take to die from starvation and dehydration?

BEATRICE FAIRBANKS CAYZER

Hours later, Myriam was using her dinner fork to try to comb her hair, when she heard the very welcome screech of a vehicle's tires.

In her desperation, even an emissary from her father would be welcome as somebody to ask for food and water.

She listened in relief and amazement to an American male voice, yelling: "Anybody home? I'll pay for water. Engine's boiling over."

"Help! Help me…" Myriam called out. "I'm imprisoned in a room near the front door. See if there's a key, I was kidnapped, and I'm being held here against my will…"

"No key anywhere." The American drew a pistol from a holster on his hip. He fired it at her door's lock, freeing Myriam, who came rushing out into the corridor.

Myriam shook her head, unbelieving that she could have escaped her captivity in time to have avoided starvation.

She barely listened to the American's questioning.

He asked: "You all right? Please tell me, what's your name?" The man obviously liked her and wanted to get into a relationship.

"I'm Myriam McLeary. But we can't stop to talk. Tell me your name later. We must leave as soon as we can. My kidnappers could come back any time."

"Kidnappers? Good god, you'd better get into my jeep."

Myriam, embarrassed that her dress missed buttons, and her hair was uncombed, didn't catch the man's signals.

He tried to clarify what his intentions were." Look, Cutie, I'm on my way to the Al-Hasa Oasis. I hope you won't dump me when we get there." After bringing water from a cistern to feed it to his engine, he revved the jeep's motor and took the route he'd memorized from his map.

"If that's okay with you, we can bunk up there together. My name's Alfred, but call me Alf. I couldn't go for a girl what called me Fred."

Keeping it to herself, she debated: "Could I survive in the desert after escaping from him?"

No. Not possible. Myriam felt that to save her baby she must play along until they reached the Oasis. After realizing the full implication of what Alf expected from her, and weighing her options, she remained silent.

Alf proved extremely talkative. His favored topics were sex, and gossip concerning divorces. "I been married and divorced twice. Married first at eighteen; what the hell, I was old enough to join the army so why not get married. The girl was no good in bed. All she wanted was a chance to wear a weddin' dress she'd bought, and go on a trip somewheres on a honeymoon. Stupid bitch thought a honeymoon. was a chance for big meals and lots to drink. Hell, she wasn't interested in goin' t'bed at all. Hey, you been married? Like goin' t'bed?"

Myriam nodded, trying to smile nicely. She couldn't bring herself to speak out to agree. When he placed his free hand on her lap, she moved toward the passenger door, but didn't dare dislodge the hand. When his fingers went on a discovery trip, she stopped him, and said: "I'm sorry but I need to go to the bathroom. Please let me go behind that tree just ahead."

Playing the gallant suitor, Alf did as was suggested, and Myriam relieved herself out of sight, taking the chance to use an open safety pin to protect the entrance to her underpants.

On her return, the jeep hit a succession of tough bumps causing Alf to keep both hands on the wheel. The road's bumps didn't slow his stream of lascivious talk. "Y'all didn't tell me if y'liked goin' t'bed. What y'prefer; top, or bottom? Front or back? I'm easy. Like it both ways."

"I'm hungry," Myriam interrupted. "Got any good American food in this jeep?"

"Hungry? For food, not for me in bed? Naughty girl! Sure, I've got a Hershey bar, a Milky Way, and some peanuts. We got a long ways t'go. Better save somepin' fo' later." He chuckled: "I always like keepin' somethin' fo' later! Get my drift?"

Myriam did get the drift, although she had no precise idea of what he was alluding to: her marital experience had been restricted to old-fashioned love making with Dennis: a man who had been in prison for seventeen years, and relieved to have what's normal.

When Alf caught up with a stalled car in front of them and asked for water for his engine, Myriam made use of the opportunity to ease out of the front passenger seat to take up a safer position in the rear of the jeep.

Back on his route to the Al-Hara oasis, Alf complained. "What's got into you, Cutie. Why the back seat? I suddenly got bad breath, or somethin'?"

"I'm feeling sick. I might vomit—or, worse—on top of you. Something I ate last night must have been bad."

"We can stop at a tree again. Do what y'have to do."

"Comes and goes." Myriam began to make a plan to rid herself of Alf. "Stop at the first restaurant in the Oasis, where there might be a public bathroom for ladies."

"'Ladies' at the Al-Hara? Not damn likely. That's where men go to get the cuties they want to sleep with. Big center for sex trafficking. But y'must know about the White Slave Trade! Why else would y'git kidnapped? How did it happen? Git chloroformed in the bathroom of a movie the-a-ter? Lots o'girls got kidnapped thet way… Happens even in Ohio, where I hails from."

"My mother and I went as tourists to the Wailing Wall in Jerusalem. I helped her get into a taxi for the railroad station for her long trip home, and then was bundled into a burqa while I waited for a bus."

"Thet man wut ordered your kidnappin' sho' ain't no generous provider. I saw y'd no bed in your room. Gotta have a bed t'screw in comfo't. Bein' personal, I'll tell you I gotta have a bed. And no new dress fo' you, in how many months? Three! I'll buy you new dresses. How many y'want?"

Alf was determined to further his self-imposed role of gallant gentleman. When they arrived at the Al-Hara Oasis, he slowed down past its lavish rows of trees to search out a first-class restaurant where foreign tourists could use its rest rooms. But if

Myriam waited a very long time in that restaurant in hopes Alf would give up on her, she proved mistaken. Alf and the jeep were waiting too near the restaurant's front entrance for her to make an escape.

Next, he stopped at a booth displaying a selection of foreign dresses. "Wut's your size?" he yelled from the booth, with a clutch of cotton clothes in his hands.

Myriam started to reply that her size was six. But, thinking of the changes to her waistline from her four months' pregnancy, she replied: "Size eight. But, please don't bother. What I need right now is another good restaurant's bathroom. I think I've got diarrhea."

His face turning grim, Alf paid for the size eight dresses he'd chosen and found another first class restaurant for Myriam. Again he was waiting—although now impatiently—for Myriam to emerge. Again she had no chance to escape from him.

He said: "I think we should head straight for the Aminoil camp. You can use a bathroom there all night. And I c'n keep my bed warm for you."

The jeep took the straight route for Kuwait and the main Aminoil camp.

On the trip, Alf reverted to his long-winded fascination with stories of sex and divorce. "I sees as you've got a weddin' ring; You've got a divorce?"

"Maybe. Right now, I'm not sure. The man who had me kidnapped warned me he was arranging one."

"Did you sleep with him?"

"No." Myriam didn't elaborate; she was fully aware that the less Alf learned about her, the safer she would be.

Alf showed he was satisfied with her reply by promptly diving into an unconfirmed story regarding actress Vivien Leigh and her second husband, Laurence Olivier. "That man's got one hell of a roving eye! How could any normal fellow look beyond the most gorgeous woman in the whole world who happens to be his wife. The whole world adored Vivien Leigh for her role as Scarlet O'Hara in GONE WITH THE WIND. But I've heard a rumor that paints her as mean. Seems like his child, Tarquin, that he'd had with his first wife, Jill Esmond, was shunted out of the marital home until custody of the boy was given totally to Jill."

"Sorry to hear that, because Vivian Leigh's one of my favorite actresses. She made me want to be a Southern American Belle. But since you know stuff about famous people, tell me what you know about Saudi Arabia's King Abdul Aziz."

"Not much. I hear he keeps his country living in the Seventh Century."

"You're right about that. Anything else?"

"He makes exceptions for friends and members of his family."

Now Myriam became truly interested. She had many questions she'd like to have answered regarding King Abdul Aziz's character. Her main interest concerned hearing the names of his friends. Was her father one of them?

"Mr. J. Paul Getty, has made the most money for him. I'll tell you about him."

Later, Myriam digested all of this soiled spate, but she regurgitated it in a surprising way. It occurred to her that Kuwait City might have a Christian church where she could go to plead for help: for food, a roof over her head, and ultimately a job. "Alf, do you know if Kuwait permits Christian churches in the country?"

"Yes, the eventual Constitution does, but the main religion is Muslim, and most laws are based on Sharia principles. Why?" Alf bristled: he was quick to sense that Myriam might be planning to escape his bed by taking sanctuary in a church. He knew she had no money, no passport, and no connections in Kuwait, which he'd originally thought would force her to fall in with his plans.

But, would she?

Myriam didn't answer his question: she changed the perilous subject of a church in Kuwait City, steering him back to talk about J. Paul Getty.

"How come he knows the King of Saudi Arabia?"

"They goes a ways back. He come to Riyadh in the mid-1930s. Probably saw the country's possibilities then. Smart man. Graduated from Berkeley in California, and Cambridge in England. Writes books. Keeps his employees long time: twenty years his butler, seventeen years his chef Catherine Aepli. Owns a gorgeous estate outside London called Sutton Place, bought from the Duke and Duchess of Sutherland.

Learned to live with beautiful things from a Palm Beach lady, Amy Phipps. Fillin' every one of his homes with great art. Folks thinks as that art is to please hisself. Ain't so. He's collectin' art to put up a museum in California for us people. But the women, that's a different story."

"In what way?"

"Three divorces already. Probably will be more. Marries, divorces. Marries, divorces. He surrounds hisself with fabulous available females. Like an old-time Arab with a harem."

"My father should have done that. He wouldn't be so cruel. He didn't even divorce my mother: she divorced him because he was lethal. I need to warn her I've escaped that house where you found me."

"There's phones and telegraph in the Aminoil camp. You can contact her. Look, we're getting close. That mountain ahead: it's the Ash-Shiqdyd Peak. Look how the sunset's colorin' rocks on its west side. All crimson 'n purple. Real nice… Don't you think?"

The camp wasn't close. It seemed a long time before they drove up to its security guards.

Alf had kept to himself that he had changed venues and decided against driving to the main camp, in favor of one closer to the Saudi Arabian border.

Myriam suspected something of the sort, but couldn't help and wonder if maybe Alf had a jealous wife or another "Cutie" already using the bed in his own camp's apartment.

Alf showed the security guard his credentials. There was a barrier across the camp's main entrance, like the ones at railroad crossings. The jeep had to stop at the barrier. "Brought along a girlfriend," Alf winked salaciously. "You guys wouldn't spoil a little fun! You've looked over my identity stuff before. You knows I can't take little missie here to my own camp. Come on! Be good sports."

The camp's barrier swung open.

Alf quickly located a bungalow with a Bedroom For Rent sign.

The landlord promptly answered the jeep's demanding horn, a deal was made and Alf gestured to Myriam that she should go into the room. It had a double bed, and a bathroom with a shower. There were no tables or closets. One solitary chair was of flimsy make, but the blackout curtains looked sturdy in spite of obviously having had plenty of use.

Myriam rushed for the shower. It had a window-sill stocked with different kinds of birth control devices.

She wished there had been a bathtub: she would have slept in it gladly if Alf would settle for the bed.

Chapter 9

Digboi, India; Saudi Arabia Desert and a Camel Racetrack, Near Riyadh

Flying over Bombay, again Dennis thought: "What a beautiful city." It straddled a great bay and had many fine government buildings left there from the recently ended days of the British rule.

But, as with Alexandria, when the experimental flight safely landed and he was being taxied to his hotel, again he saw lepers, and many homeless children sifting through garbage heaped in the streets hoping for something still edible.

His Orange Tree Hotel lived up to its name with an entry drive studded by orange trees standing like sentinels before a palace. His room had an en suite bathroom with hot and cold water, a bathtub with plentiful towels, and an alcove offering packets of coffee or tea.

What most impressed him at night were the neatly positioned shoes outside each guest's door waiting to be polished for use the next morning.

He didn't see much of Bombay before going to the railroad station to catch his train for Digboi City. What he did see was a flamboyant parade by a Regiment of British soldiers leaving India. It was organized to impress: the officers wore glistening armor from hips to shoulders, topped by silver colored plumed helmets—a great spectacle.

The Digboi Company had issued Dennis a Second Class ticket. That did not include meals.

Dennis decided to forego the dining car, and made do with food sold through his open window by vendors on the platforms of his route.

Melmut, on the same train, complained grimly. "What a welcome. I hate eating out of a window. When I was a child and my father took me by train from Alexandria to Cairo, we ate the food sold that way and we both got paratyphoid."

He cheered up on arrival at Digboi, because a youngish stylish British woman was doing a Personnel job greeting incoming workers and executives.

She singled out Dennis, looking past Melmut to hold the American's hand an overlong time then thrusting her arm into the crook of his elbow. "I'm Aimee Crawley," she said. "Aimee, for loving, of course. Come on, I've organized a rickshaw. I'll take you to my club. I apologize about the Second

Class ticket, someone in the office must have goofed."

Dennis treading carefully, unused to such a flagrant invite to a flirtation, said: "That's okay. Glad to be here."

"Over to your right is where I live. Second floor, in the white building. Want to come in for a coffee?"

"No. Can't. Got a letter I must post." To change the subject to one less inflammatory, Dennis continued: "I'd appreciate it if you'd tell me some highlights about where we are. Things for which the area's best known."

Her grin thinning from obvious frustration, Aimee nevertheless complied.

She thought she'd caught a live one on her line and decided to be pleasant while she reeled him in." Digboi is in one of the Seven Sisters provinces. Digboi itself has been pumping oil since it was discovered here in the late eighteen hundreds. Among the provinces there are different claims to fame, such as having the oldest and largest Buddhist Monastery in India, and a holy Sanctuary to cure any ills. Personally, I'd recommend my own bed as the best sanctuary."

Reddening with discomfort, Dennis asked: "What's the gray building ahead?"

"My club. Founded by British officers stationed here who needed to make sure the oil supply wouldn't be sabotaged. Especially important during the two World Wars."

"Could we wait to go in until my colleague's rickshaw catches up with us?"

"Colleague? That little brown Egyptian? He can't come in with us. Club's only for Whites. And how can you call him a colleague?"

"We both have contracts guaranteeing us pay at $32 a day," Dennis muttered lamely.

Aimee rediscovered her pushy smile. "Only $32 a day? For a man like you!

Come see me in my office tomorrow, and I'll finagle much better. Also guaranteed."

The rickshaw stopped at the main door of her club. Aimee paid, with a wry grin intimating that Dennis wouldn't have any currency as low as a rupee, and with one hand in his marched triumphantly into a very grand front room crowded with oil executives.

Within minutes it became apparent that most of the men knew Aimee in the Biblical sense. She was showing off the new catch she'd made.

Dennis accepted a quick coffee, but ordered a rickshaw with the steward's help. He gave his address for the steward to repeat, explaining that he didn't know the local language.

"Oh Sir, there are over twenty of those. You'll make do with English for most things."

Aimee's frosty goodbye came with an addition: "I can teach you Hindustani if you come to my place after hours. See you tomorrow in my office?"

Dennis nodded, and climbed into his rickshaw. Alone, he squirmed recalling the pornographic parts of his welcome.

He hadn't stopped longing for Myriam, not for a moment.

The next morning, after checking in with a supervisor and getting his orders for the afternoon, he called in at Aimee's office.

Very business-like, Aimee had dropped her inviting tone by an octave. "How are you? Better, now that you've settled in and sent the all-important letter?"

"Better, thanks. Funny-tummy, but otherwise fine. I nodded I'd call in."

"Aren't you going to ask me how I got you a raise to $59 an hour, and the rest of the morning off?"

"That was your doing!"

"I thought I'd show you a few local marvels." Again she produced a rickshaw. Again it was meant for one passenger: providing an opportunity for her left hip to wiggle suggestively next to Dennis's right one.

The first marvel included a visit to the closest Buddhist Monastery to view its pornographic images cut into a stone wall. "Instructive, wouldn't you say?" inquired Aimee, like a kitten about to enjoy catnip.

Dennis couldn't reply. He was too busy trying to blot out the images as relating to Aimee.

Before he'd succeeded in blotting out all the images, their rickshaw had deposited Dennis and Aimee at her apartment building.

While entering, Aimee had been perfuming her ears, neck and the cleavage between her breasts. In the elevator to the Second Floor, she pressed her entire body against Dennis, whispering: "SHALL I GIVE YOU YOUR FIRST LESSONS IN HINDUSTANI?"

When the elevator door opened Dennis tried to make a run to escape, but Aimee pulled him into her foyer.

It smelled strongly of her perfume, and of woman.

Aimee speedily removed her clothes, including pants and brassiere, while managing to light candles situated next to her open double bed.

She lay down, lifted her legs, and stretched out her arms lasciviously.

Without a word, Dennis turned on his heels and dashed for her front door. He kept running, eschewing the elevator preferring the stairs, and never slowed down until he huffed into his own mini-apartment.

Three months passed during which Dennis successfully avoided Aimee. He used the laborer's unpretentious club. He took lessons from a pimpled boy called Henry: the lessons were to teach him to speak and read Arabic.

The only time he saw Aimee again was one sultry evening when he was sitting outside his building studying a Dictionary with Henry. Aimee created a hateful scene. She stopped her rickshaw and, after giving Henry a piercing look, said: "Now I understand why you turned me down! Obviously, you prefer boys…"

Her comment hit Dennis between his legs. His Dictionary fell into the mud. Henry, his cheeks as red as a Himalayan sunset, retrieved the Dictionary, and grunted: "No more lessons, Mr. McLeary. I'm not a queer and I don't want people thinking I am. Too bad you were only halfway through Arabic grammar!"

Dennis, later, alone in his room, debated leaving Digboi. He still needed the generous salary, if he hoped to pay for the eight hour flight to Saudi Arabia with a commercial airline.

At his darkest moment, Mehmet called from outside. "Dennis, I've got incredible news. Might lead to Myriam. Come on to the club. There's someone you must meet."

The so-called laborers' club was cozy and welcoming. Seated in a wicker armchair, looking out for Mehmet, was a keiling half-breed. Centuries of the occupying British soldiers in India had resulted in thousands of mixed-breed children who didn't know where they belonged. Some had blonde hair and blue eyes mixed with dark skin. The light skinned ones often had hook noses and caramel eyes. Many of both kinds had been abused sexually.

Dennis recognized a fellow victim the moment they met.

"I'm Dennis McLeary," he said, holding out his right hand while he pulled up a chair with his left. "I hear you may have some important news for me."

"My name is Frances Patel. I've spent most of my life tending camels for any British regiments that used camels. Last week I was offered a job to be groom to a famous camel that has won many races: some as far away as in Australia. The British officer, who raced him is leaving for Scotland, so he sold this great camel to a civilian who now wants to sell him on to a Saudi prince: one of the sons of the king. Much money is involved. But I must get to the news for you. This camel, name of DESTINY, is losing his groom: who just arrived here from Riyadh with his charge. Among the many stories of this groom he told of one Youssef, a former camel jockey, who now manages a mansion far out into the northern desert. This Youssef claims that there is a Turkish woman there being held in a locked room. He knows she is Turkish because she speaks Arabic with a Turkish accent. Youssef has been forbidden to speak to her, but she often pleads for water. Mehmet thought she could be your half-Turkish wife, who is missing."

"Thank you. How can I find out?"

"DESTINY's groom has quit. His wife is having a baby, so DESTINY is without a groom. Not good. He is scheduled to race outside Riyadh in a few days. The job has been offered to me, but I broke a leg and am still recovering. Take this job. You will be flown by private plane; no expenses spared. Mehmet will come with you."

"But I don't know anything about tending a camel. I don't have an Indian passport. And I don't speak Arabic."

"I can give you a raw idea of what to do. I can produce a forger for a fake passport. As for the language, Mehmet suggested you pass yourself off as a deaf mute."

"In my Florida job, I did groom Mr. Blunt's horses. Is there a big difference? And as for being a mute, I often wish I'd kept my mouth shut."

"Mehmet suggested you dye your hair black, grow a stubble and dye it black too."

"Okay."

'HE ALSO SUGGESTED YOU BUY USED CLOTHES A GROOM HAD WORN. No! Better... You must go to DESTINY's old groom and beg him for clothes he can spare. Slippers, head dress, everything. Do not mix these with any of your own clothes. A camel has a keen sense of smell. Can smell water that's miles away."

"Can you take me to DESTINY's groom? Now?"

"Yes. Mehmet, ask for two rickshaws."

Frances had a six-year-old son who appeared alongside one of the rickshaws. The boy acted as a crutch for his father, who did have difficulty walking.

At the home of DESTINY's groom, a celebration was in progress. His baby had been born a few hours ago: his first. He was almost abrupt when asked for his old clothes. But remembering to thank Allah for the great gift of a son, he parted with one full set, including a tarboosh.

Next, Dennis went to a barber and had his hair dyed black. For his stubble, eyebrows and eyelashes he used women's cosmetics for the black color.

Fully dressed in the stinking clothes, Dennis was introduced to DESTINY, who snuggled up to him instantly.

"Looks like I'm slated to be a camel's pet. I just hope he flies well in a small airplane. Wouldn't be fun if he spits all over me."

"You'll have no problem with DESTINY. It's his Owner who's difficult. Shouldn't be. Wealthy already, he's going to be paid a fortune by the Prince, and in addition— if DESTINY wins—he gets to keep the winning prize, which is $50,000. But, he's a greedy one. Who knows what else he'll try to wrangle in Riyadh."

Dennis met DESTINY's Owner at the airport. This was his first meeting, but when he got a look at him in the light, he recognized a type he'd met many times in prison.

He resolved to keep his distance whenever possible.

In the Saudi Arabian Customs shed at Riyadh, DESTINY's Owner disclaimed any connection to Dennis.

"Groom to my camel? Never saw him before. But then, DESTINY has had a succession of grooms recently."

When it looked as if Dennis was to be expelled within minutes of his arrival, the Saudi prince—who craved winning the next day's big race—appeared in the shed.

In perfect English, he scolded: "Who is impeding this man's entry?"

The Custom's shed chief officer cringed at the prince's tone. "Only doing my job, Your Royal Highness. This son of filth claims to be from Digboi, but he wears a Tarboosh."

"You won't have a job if you cause trouble. Stamp his visa."

"Your Royal Highness, he has a duffle bag containing T-shirts and bluejeans. What groom—"

"Gifts for other grooms. Stamp his visa."

"Your Royal Highness, his Indian passport claims he is a deaf-mute. What need has Saudi Arabia of another such? "

"Allah wishes us to be merciful. Give me that rubber stamp. I'll stamp his passport." The prince didn't acknowledge Dennis: too low on the totem pole. He strolled out of the Customs shed, eagerly inquiring of the Owner whether DESTINY had traveled well.

Dennis, who had learned to keep out of the way in prison when trouble was brewing, followed them well behind, toting his duffle bag. The prince and DESTINY's Owner oversaw a calmed DESTINY being installed in a British-made horse box, with Dennis crouched alongside.

The prince's facilities for his camels proved to be as comfortable as those for horses preparing to run at Ascot, which belonged to the British royals and that no doubt the prince had visited.

Dennis, along with dozens of other grooms, had a room to himself, and a shower. He shouldn't make use of the shower, he knew. DESTINY liked his stink as it was.

Dinnertime, Dennis scoured the supper-room to locate any other English-speaking grooms. There was a close-knit group in one corner laughing at English jokes. One joke made Dennis smile, but he smothered the corresponding laugh because that could give him away.

Eating quietly nearby, he used his jailtime know-how to weigh the character of each of the merrymakers, finally resolving to go to the tallest man's room after dinner.

Following him to his door, he gestured without speaking to ask if he could come in.

"Hi, I'm Andy." The man had an Australian accent. He showed no surprise that this malodorous groom would want to enter. "Is it that you want a drink? No alcohol allowed in Saudi country." The tall man settled in his one chair with a glass of lemonade.

Dennis entered and he carefully shut the door. But before introducing himself and explaining his reason for being there, he made his intentions clear. Dennis wanted the man to know promptly this was not a homosexual's come on. He didn't want a repeat of the mistake concerning Henry.

"No, thanks; no drink: I'm trying to find my wife. She was kidnapped by Saudi thugs three—no, four—months ago. I love her beyond life itself. I need someone to help me find her. I don't speak Arabic, and anyway I'm supposed to be a deaf mute. Could you—"

"Help you? That I don't know." Andy showed no surprise that this uninvited visitor spoke English with an American accent. "But lots of the grooms here have heard about a young Turkish woman being held in a house in the northern desert."

"Lots of grooms? How can that be?"

The tall Australian unscrambled his legs like a marionette on strings. "Man who runs that house—name of Youssef—is an ex camel-jockey. He hangs around the races. Talks."

"Yes. That's what I heard. Why I'm here. I'm groom for DESTINY. On the card for tomorrow's big race. His former groom told that story way off in India."

"Damn fool, get killed if he doesn't shut up. I've been invited to the desert house by Youssef. Put off going. I don't look for trouble, and I have a gut feeling there could be a dangerous confrontation there. Just my luck to go on the wrong day."

"How about tomorrow?"

"Nope. Got to be on tap for the big race. But, say, when the races are over we might have a clear chance of getting there without being followed. Folks celebrating a win, maybe, and wanting to stay at the race course. Come see me. I might give it a try. Yeah, and what did you say your name was?"

"Dennis McLeary. Has to be tomorrow, because if my camel doesn't win ,I'll be booted out of the country."

Dennis spent a heartless night, tossing and turning at the thought that Myriam might be close by.

DESTINY's day dawned in a promising way. The camel had got over the fatigue from flying, and sensed he was going to race. He was a schooled athlete that reveled in his sport. Playing games with Dennis, he gave little kicks to prod him toward the waiting racing colors.

DESTINY, at ten feet in length and seven feet at his shoulders, felt cramped in his box. Yet in the cool of night he'd missed the warmth of Dennis's body.

Dennis started his daily work by checking that DESTINY's urine looked concentrated. He collected the healthy-looking dry feces and put them in the neat receptacle provided for that purpose. He took the wire brush and smoothed DESTINY's short hairs on his underbelly and proceeded on with the entire pelt. He even plucked the sand from the corner of DESTINY's brown eyes, because the racing camels got marks for beauty in a separate pageant.

No food or water was permitted before a race. Instead, Dennis patted and hugged his charge. In the early morning the silence was great enough to hear desert larks sing. But, after sun-up, the chattering of human voices took over until race time when they grew to a tidal wave.

When the Owner's racing handlers arrived in his stall to take DESTINY for him to be saddled, the men discovered that he wouldn't budge without having Dennis to walk beside him. Like a thoroughbred racehorse with a pet, this camel wanted to show off when it counted.

The Owner's two handlers relented and bent the rules to permit a groom to be in the saddling-up.

"We had no choice," the men apologized to the overstrung Owner, who appeared late and was more sulky than usual.

"Look at the pads of his feet! His toes haven't been cleaned." The Owner barked. "They haven't been touched…" He took Dennis by the shoulders and had started to shake him when all the men heard a warning hiss from DESTINY. The camel aimed spit at the Owner, who had to be restrained by a handler from hitting him.

Into that tension strolled His Royal Highness, all smiles and enjoying his day of racing.

"What's going on?" he asked, still basking in his own good humor. "I can see that DESTINY is in great form for his big race. Such an athlete!" Without another word, he took DESTINY's reins to lead him to the start. Dennis, unobtrusively, like a shadow kept close distance.

From the race's first moment it was evident that DESTINY was in control. Allowing his jockey to use the tactic of lingering a brief few minutes while a group of contenders alternated in the lead, when DESTINY was given his head he plunged into rocket-form to break the speed record and to win the race.

The entire huge crowd of racegoers watched as His Royal Highness passed two readied checks to the now former Owner and led DESTINY to receive the prize.

Disgruntled not to be invited to share the moment, DESTINY's former Owner had to put on an act that he was satisfied to get the checks, one for selling him, and the other for his share of the prize money of $50,000.

Dennis kept to his role of shadow, in order to spare His Royal Highness the embarrassment of watching his new champion abandon him for a groom.

When the corresponding celebration ended, DESTINY had his chance to meet Dennis's eyes for the look of congratulation he craved.

He got it, in full measure, with more pats and hugs, back in his quiet stall.

Andy was in a corner there, waiting for Dennis.

"Congrats," he said. "I hope you got a damn good tip ."

Dennis shook his head. Nothing.

"In America," Andy continued, "a jockey gets ten percent of the win. A groom would get one hell of a tip for a race worth $50,000."

Whispering, not to be overheard, Dennis commented: "I'll be lucky if that ex-Owner doesn't sell knowledge of my whereabout to agents of Myriam's father."

"Speaking of Myriam, I came here in a hurry to tell you something important. I've just seen Youssef's wife and daughter be stopped by the Religious Police for being in a mixed crowd without a male family member. They were eating at a food tent, and flirting with the owner, when they were apprehended. This is very serious in Saudi Arabia. While many at the races well knew how Youssef is a regular, he wasn't here when it mattered."

"And?"

"Youssef has to deal with this. Maybe he can spirit his women away to his Bedouin tribe out of the reach of Sharia Law. If the women can't escape sentencing, then Youssef—because he is of the Ariza tribe—Youssef and his women could still be saved by the Arizas, who might pay off a magistrate. But that's Youssef's problem. It's our chance to go see if this socalled woman is your Myriam."

"You got a vehicle?"

"No chance. And don't want to be had up for stealing one. Could be beheaded for a crime like that. But, you are A CELEBRITY AMONG THE GROOMS HERE. One of them will surely let us borrow a couple of no-hopers. Reins and saddles too. Meet you outside the gates. Be quick."

"I don't know how to ride a camel."

"Learn on our way. No other option."

Andy sneaked out of the overnight-policed stall, while Dennis pretended to DESTINY that he would be going out as usual for his brief meal.

He grabbed a coffee in the food hall, accepting congratulations as would be expected, then with his ever-ready duffle bag met Andy at a hidden enclave beyond the racecourse's gates. To Dennis's surprise, Mehmet had added himself to the venture. He'd brought a camel from the stall of another Owner, well fitted with reins, saddle, and a gourd of water.

A difficult moment hindered their departure. Although Andy had brought a short ladder-like contrivance to help Dennis into his mount's saddle, it wasn't helpful enough. Andy had to dismount from his camel to give Dennis a mighty shove. "I hope I remember how to get to Youssef's," he growled.

After three false starts, Andy got out his compass and eventually, following the hours' long trek, the three tired men saw the glint of tiled roofs.

Would Myriam be the Turkish woman in that house?

Dennis brought his camel to what was the door man of Myriam's Grandmother's house. He saw it was wide open. Rushing inside, he found Myriam's empty room.

Exhausted from the long camel-ride, Dennis sank down on the cushions that had served as her bed. He found one of her red hairs caught between two cushions, and brought it to his lips. The atmosphere was full of her presence.

He knew he'd missed finding her by only a few hours.

Mehmet was calling from outside. "There are recent tracks of a vehicle. The tracks left two trails. The vehicle came from Riyadh. It left here for the Al-Hasa Oasis."

His heart beating rapidly, Dennis left Myriam's room to meet the unexpected sight of Mehmet remounting his camel. He shouted: "I'm heading back to Riyadh. You and Andy will have to handle everything from now on." And without further explanation, Mehmet rode for Riyadh.

Meanwhile, Andy had scooped up a worn map that lay next to the vehicle's recent tire tracks. It was a map showing the route from Kuwait to the Al-Hasa Oasis.

In turn, Dennis and Andy mounted their camels. Andy used the map he'd found to guide their way to the Al-Hasa Oasis. Dennis, his heart's pain easing, began to feel hopeful.

Eventually, with their legs aching and hands extremely stiff from all their handling of the camels' reins, Dennis and Andy did reach their destination: the legendary and beautiful tree—studded Al-Hasa Oasis.

Dennis felt anxious due to the vast numbers of foreign tourists and Saudis shoving one another throughout the nearby shopping area. Speaking low, he said: "Good grief, Andy, it's going to be like looking for a grain of sand on a beach to locate Myriam among all these people. But, we'll have to tether our camels, and make a start.:"

"No, I can't help you with that. Tether our camels? They'll be stolen the minute we turn our backs. I've got to return these good troopers from where I got them. You go searching for your Myriam. I'm heading for the prince's racing camels' facilities. But before you make a start, could you do me a favor and exchange clothes? I'd really appreciate getting your job and becoming DESTINY's groom, and it won't happen if I don't wear those stinking clothes he loves."

Andy, after changing clothes with Dennis, left to return from where they'd started. He took the reins of both the camels he'd borrowed. He chirped: "See ya, Bloke."

With a wave of his free hand, Andy was gone.

Dennis, his bones protesting, combed through hundreds of bargain hunters, then headed for an area of feasting tourists where there were restaurants.

No Myriam.

Desperate, Dennis went up to any friendly looking foreigner and showed his passport with its picture of Myriam.

No luck.

Nightfall was approaching, thinning the crowds. Shops and restaurants closed. Feeling at his wits end, Dennis was about to catch a bus for the border with Kuwait, when he caught a glimmer of interest in his story in the eyes of an elderly American woman.

She was attentively escorted by an oilman in a yellowing Panama hat, who wore a wedding ring. Apparently, he was her husband. She said: "I'm very touched by your story, and so is my husband. He works for the Gulf Oil Company, in Kuwait. Gulf's expanding facilities on its share of the Neutral Zone, going to explore in the off-shore PZ. You know about that? Kuwait's not far from here. You could come home with us and pass the border as our son."

Dennis, halfway through an apologetic excuse, looked through a crowd of Saudis to see Mehmet emerging from the limousine and taking cash from a newly arrived businessman: his former boss, DESTINY's ex-Owner. It was a lot of cash.

Mehmet!

Dennis realized immediately that Mehmet had sold him for the amount needed to pay off the mortgage on Iliana's Alexandria apartment.

After quickly reconsidering the offer to go to Kuwait with the elderly couple, Dennis took the woman's arm and urged her to hurry to a 1937 Chevrolet that had a Kuwait license. "Yes. Thanks, let's get going." He blurted,"I'm grateful for the invitation."

Dennis ducked down behind the Chevrolet's front seats and hoped the woman could take to the road before the Chevrolet could be followed. "Our names? I prefer Suzy, and my husband is just plain

Henry. Call us what you like. I wouldn't mind it, though, if you called me "Little Mother.' Hal prefers 'Pop.'"

Many miles later, with no sign of being tailed, the Chevrolet made it past the security guards of the Gulf Oil concession. There had been no query as to Dennis's lack of a visa: Suzy had yelled out her window: "We done brought back our boy with us."

Myriam, towelling herself having left the shower in the Gulf Oil Concession's bungalow, heard a gentle rapping on the cottage door. She looked into the bedroom, and to her amazement saw Alf kneeling on the floor with his forehead pressed against its bare boards.

"I'm at my night prayers, I'm Russian Orthodox and I pray every night before bed," he explained, and began a recitation of the Lord's Prayer in Russian: "Otche Nash."

There was a repeat of the gentle rapping on their door, interrupting Alf's first few words, but he didn't make any effort to answer the rapping. Myriam crouched to go around him to answer. She opened it to find a middle-aged lady, completely outfitted in Quaker-gray: no ornaments for relief, offering a welcome trolley with two dinners, including slices of chocolate cake.

No sign of any drinks. "No alcohol allowed in Kuwait," the lady quietly explained. "And as I am a Quaker, and we don't permit alcohol either, you have to do without."

Myriam looked past the lady.

A 1937 Chevrolet was barreling along in the street outside. There were three passengers: an elderly couple in the front seats, while her black-bearded Dennis was crushed between bags of groceries in the rear.

Myriam gasped in ecstasy. She yelled: "Dennis, DENNIS!"

At the sound of her voice, he swiveled his head like a billiard ball aiming for a pocket, and their eyes locked.

The Chevrolet pushed on like a horse bolting to its barn for its oats.

Dressed in nothing more than the towel, Myriam resisted racing after the car.

Awash with soaring emotions, she turned her attention to the Quaker lady, who droned on as if there had been no explosion of intense desire for Dennis from Myriam.

"There's no coca cola in the commissary or I'd have brought some: there's been none for a month now. And the water here is disgusting. Sorry. May I come in? My name's Beryl Waites. What's yours?"

"Yes, yes. Thank you so much..." Myriam turned on her good manners, like urging water from a faulty faucet. "My name's Myriam McLeary. Do come in. You'll have to by-pass my friend. He's at his 'evening prayers. Christian prayers."

Myriam gestured toward the only chair. She said: "Do sit down. I'll just be a minute. I want to change out of this wet towel."

She hurried to the bathroom, where she had hung the Brown dress worn in Jerusalem to please Mommy, and which she hadn't been able to change out of during the past three months. It was open over the stomach.

After the long ride to Kuwait, its buttons were finally no longer able to contain her bulging stomach. The gap clearly exposed her four months' pregnancy.

"How lovely. I see you've joined the club," Beryl exclaimed heartily on Myriam's reappearance "This baby going to be your first?"

Ravenous for food, Myriam waited to swallow the meat in a sandwich before replying. Also, she was still hesitant to make any explanation for her shouts of DENNIS! "Yes, my first. Is there a doctor in this camp? I haven't seen a doctor yet, for a check-up."

"Not many pregnant women here. You'd do better to have a real obstetrician have a look. I could drive you to Medina. That's in Saudi Arabia, of course. Very busy right now, what with Hajj going on. Over a million pilgrims this year! I'd like to see the great Black Rock. But I'm a Friend, meaning a Quaker, and I don't believe they allow Christians anywhere near the Hajj."

Having completed his prayers, Alf listened attentively. He was extremely keen to learn the answer to Myriam's shouts of DENNIS! But, after introducing himself as an employee of the local oil company, he threw in a piece of information that exploded in the room with as much emotional impact as if he had been a suicide bomber. "This lady has recently been the victim of a kidnapping. I helped her escape from a sealed room where she'd been held for three months. She'd have died within days for lack of drinking water, after being left alone in that locked room, if I hadn't found her."

Then he took one of the dinner plates, plunked a sandwich on it and proceeded to eat as if he had said nothing more important than that Myriam had come out of Saudi Arabia from a shopping trip.

Beryl listened aghast. Her smile vanished. She dabbed at her eyes, although there were no tears. She said, gasping: "I've never known anyone before who had been kidnapped. What can I do to help you, Myriam?"

At that moment, a heavily breathing Dennis appeared in the doorway, Andy's clothes thoroughly drenched in sweat. "Myriam! My darling! My wife!" He slurred from exhaustion but rushed across the crowded bedroom to take Myriam into his arms. "Thank god, thank God,": he repeated over and over.

"Dennis!" Myriam offered her lips for a long kiss. Dennis's dyed black hair and beard didn't deter her for a second.

Primly, Beryl broke into the magic. "I assume you are the husband! My offer holds. How can I help?"

Now shaking from the thought of her father's horrific revenge on anyone who helped her, Myriam pulled away from Dennis, pleading: "We should all stay here in Kuwait. You, too, Dennis. Especially you. My father's thirst for vengeance will mean the beheading of anyone who helped me. If need be, I guess I should return to Grandma's desert house so that my father will leave you in peace. Stop any more beheadings."

Beryl shook her grey head. "No. You must consider your baby."

"Baby!" Shouting with joyful exuberance, Dennis slipped a hand to Myriam's waist. He felt the buttonholes that had been torn open and realized the significance. His joy overwhelmed him. "Myriam, my precious wonderful darling! You'd wanted a baby so much! And it's coming?"

Myriam, joining him in joy, gave a tiny giggle: "Not quite yet! Baby's got another few more months to arrive."

Beryl broke in again:"Mr. McLeary, did you bring your passport, with Myriam's picture in it?"

Dennis pointed to his rolled-up, bedraggled duffle bag which he'd thrown on the floor, having brought it with him from the Chevrolet. He muttered "Thank god, yes. The camel that brought me to the oasis had a Bedouin's hold-all big enough for it to fit into. Yes, my passport, but there's no visa for Saudi Arabia, nor for Kuwait. Let me be frank: I'd been in prison for seventeen years and have no wish to go back. Paid 'my debt to society' as Myriam well knows. We entered Alexandria, in Egypt, okay. Captain of the DEVERON, the ship we were married on: he made it all legal. Later, we walked across the Egypt-Israeli border the day after Israel became a nation. Myriam, kidnapped by Saudi agents for her father, was flown by private plane to a secret landing strip in Saudi Arabia. She has a Saudi Arabian passport; no visa needed. I got a job with an oil company that provided me with a visa for India. There, I took the job of a camel's groom for a temporary entry to Saudi Arabia. But we're illegal here in Kuwait."

Myriam added: "My father ordered the beheading of my Great-aunt for helping me to join Dennis. Now, I'm concerned ever since for anybody who helps us."

Dennis returned to the story to elaborate: "I saw the blood after the beheading of the two women in a swimming suit shop who had offered Myriam a job."

Myriam's joyful expression vanished to be displaced by tears of horror. "No! Not also those two kind girls in the shop! And my father has been threatening that my mother would be beheaded if I didn't go home with him. Just to make sure, he had me taken to

Saudi Arabia in a rug. I almost suffocated. It's a miracle our baby didn't die."

Alf intervened: "I got me an idea," he paused to pick grit from a tooth: "Beryl, here, she said like she's wantin' to go t'Kuwait City and maybe help Myriam see a specialist there. Beryl, has you got a visa for Kuwait? Specific-like, from a port area?" Alf pushed on: "Mr. Maclery , since you been in prison, y'must have heard tell about them guys what can fake stuff on passports. Some guy what could change Beryl's picture fo' Myriam's."

Beryl didn't comment. She unslung her strappy handbag and produced her passport. "Take a look. I believe everything is in order. One problem, Myriam and I have an age difference of at least twenty years.'" She laughed gently. "There is another important point: I'm not pregnant."

"Some women look real young for their age." Alf broke in again. "Pregnant? I bought some bigger size dresses for her. Myriam's pregnancy won't show. After all, I never guessed she was preggers."

Beryl turned pensive. She kept her body ninety percent under control, except for her hands that trembled like bull-rushes in a storm. With her voice unsteady, Beryl followed with an idea along the lines of Alf's optimism: "Myriam and her husband can get out of the Gulf area on a freighter from one of the city's ports. Go somewhere safe."

Myriam took Beryl's free hand. "You really are a friend, in every meaning of the word. I can never thank you enough: but I'm going to take you up on your offer. Dennis, this gives us a chance to keep our baby. If I go back to my father, he's sure to order an abortion. He won't permit a little Dennis McLeary to be among his descendants."

"Our baby! Oh my gosh, thank you, Beryl. And thank you, my darling wonder of a wife, for being so brave to try to pass for a Quaker in Muslim ports."

Beryl prepared to leave. First, she said: "When I was a little girl living in Ashland, Pennsylvania there was no Friends Meeting House. We had two movie theaters, the Roxy and The Temple, an A&P for groceries, and a drugstore. My folks drove me to Harrisburg, three hours away, to go to Meeting. I was scared of cars, but I'd felt safe if I could sing my favorite songs. So, although I was going to Meeting to seek out my Inner Light, my folks would let me sing all the way to Harrisburg and back. I hope you know lots of songs: I hope you find your Inner Light."

On that note, after a loving hug from Myriam, Beryl pushed her empty welcome wagon out the doorway. It was empty, because Dennis had gleefully helped himself to the two slices of chocolate cake.

Alf said: "I'll drive y'two to Kuwait City in my jeep. But let's us get goin' right now; easier to get past the guards at night. The two of y'can catch up on your sleep in the back seat. But, before you load your duffle bag, dig out your passport, if that's where it's kept. And don't call the capital by its Kuwaiti name, 'cause y'll give us away. This is still a British Protectorate."

"Got it." Dennis handed over the all-important passport which he'd stored as usual in his duffle bag.. He tossed the nearly-empty duffle bag on the floor of Alf's jeep, and tenderly turned to help Myriam, who was stumbling into the vehicle.

Chapter 10

Kuwait City and the Strait of Hormuz

At the end of their journey to Kuwait City, Dennis had to make use of several more of the ploys he'd learned in prison.

First, he checked on what remained of his $10,000 through a Kuwaiti bank; critical because Dennis's account was nearly on empty.

Alf, who existed from paycheck to paycheck, left Myriam and Dennis on Kuwait City's main street, at the door of an unimposing hotel. He didn't offer money, he didn't expect to receive any. Alf didn't wave a goodbye. He wore his most grim expression as he drove away without regaling Myriam and Dennis to one of his extra-long speeches. His roundtrip in search of a willing "Cutie' had proved as fruitless as a desert tree. Alf, after his involvement with a kidnapping and an exchange of passports, left Kuwait City for his camp, home, and wife.

Hours later, when both Myriam and Dennis emerged from their tiny bedroom, their ecstatic expressions were like those of newlyweds on a honeymoon.

They were wearing outfits totally acceptable in this Muslim city. Myriam's oasis-bought sleeveless above -the-knee shift might have been shocking in Riyadh. But here in Kuwait, it didn't cause a single frown. To their astonishment, there were no women in a hijab. Dennis looked normal in a T-shirt and blue jeans. Very few men wore turbans or the Saudi checkered head-dress.

Police garb, on some of its streets, belonged in an English village. The policemen, handling traffic, wore the tall navy blue helmets of British policemen in Britain.

Dennis made what was nearly his first call to the Kuwait bank best known for handling Americans' funds, where Dennis scraped to empty the last remaining funds from his National City account that had duly been deposited in July by Deedee Murray Pierce.

Next, Dennis brought Myriam with him when using his prison know-how to locate a reliable forger to exchange her photo for Beryl's on the all-important new passport.

By mid-afternoon the couple decided to go sightseeing to appear like normal tourists.

They settled on taking a bus to view the city's remnants of its ancient Greek era.

An American with a Brooklyn accent— another fake tourist—also in blue jeans and T-shirt, pushed himself against Dennis, whispering: "Where the hell does a man get a real drink around here?"

Dennis grinned before he replied. He welcomed the sound of a Brooklyn accent after Alf's Ohio drawl. "No chance. YOU'D BE FINED BEFORE THE FIRST SIP. Come back on the bus with us and I'll get you one at our hotel. Not the most elegant place, but secretly serves real drinks to foreigners. Otherwise, you'll have to be invited to the U.S.A. Consulate. Get all you want, there, unless you hit on a snobby diplomat."

Myriam asked: "You American?"

"In my own way, I am. As you can tell, born in Brooklyn. But first of all, I'm a Muslim. Just the same, call me Herb."

"That doesn't sound very Muslim."

"After five years in prison, I altered it from Holi. Fed up with being made fun of, because I'm definitely not holy. You here with an American party? Got the easy-visies for Saudi Arabia? Easy, when you pay nine thousand ollars to a travel agent in New York who specializes in getting American Muslims to the Hajj. You two are going to Mecca?"

"No. And I'm not sure we'll stick around to see more Persian Gulf countries either. I'm not a Muslim. I understand there's a big fine and deportation if you get caught in places forbidden to non-believers in Saudi Arabia. Worse, you can lose a hand, or even your head for stealing, or adultery. There's Honor Killings, too. Those Saudis don't want to lose their women to infidels. But tell us why you went to prison."

"Oh, that? I was caught for speeding at 100 miles an hour in a school zone. Stupid New Jersey cop. He'd missed me when I was going 120 miles an hour. I told him off, and that cost me the extra two years. I had to beat off buggerers the whole five years."

Dennis's grin had vanished with this litany. He broke into it, fast: "There's our bus. We want to catch it for the return trip to our hotel. You taking me up on that drink I offered?"

"Sure." Herb clarified his reply by taking a seat next to Myriam on their bus. The seat was directly behind Dennis's. Herb kept up his banter regarding the Hajj, although criticism of it—even in a liberal country like British-controlled Kuwait—could be risking jailtime, or worse. "My uncle paid my Brooklyn travel agent nine thousand for me, and I was offered the use of his plane to get to Medina. Sure, I'd have liked to see the one million pilgrims circling the great Black Stone. But who wants to fast during the daytime for thirty days? No food, no drinks! Not me… And you can't even cut your fingernails. Which means no sex. I'm not one to have sex with shaggy fingernails."

Myriam made a thing out of staring out the window. Dennis kept his comments for later when he'd be alone with Myriam.

Herb persisted in acting badly. His compliments were worse than his criticisms. Suddenly he tweeked at the back of Dennis's head, pulling out some hairs. "I like your look," he said.

Dennis gave this Brooklyn stranger a second up-and-down. Could he be soliciting sodomy?"

Herb wiped out that suspicion with three words. "I want women. Lots of women. Sometimes twice a day, but always every day."

Myriam cut in. "Let's forget about drinks at our hotel. The whole idea was a mistake. We haven't time to lose. Dennis, we should get out of Kuwait as soon as possible. My father—"

Dennis nodded. He said nothing, however he gave a cautionary warning with a finger to his lips. What did they really know about this Brooklyn Muslim?

Herb interrupted: "Great idea. We'll all three leave Kuwait, soonest. Why stay when a place has nothing more to offer as a great treat than a few Greek-era stones? Hell, I don't need it. I'll go to Greece and see the Parthenon that has grace and beauty. Plus, its women are super sexy. Come with me. Could be great fun."

Oh?. "My Uncle bought a plane from the local oil company. This one can go down into a small space like a helicopter. You must have seen those oil fields where derricks are crowded like infantrymen going into battle. Oil companies need these special planes that can land in them Uncle said I could take it any time."

Dennis hesitated. This invitation came from an individual who was very different from Little Mother.

It was Myriam who made an about-face and speedily accepted Herb's offer.

"Fine. But do we need vaccinations? A different visa?"

"Hell! No. Uncle—a relation on my Mom's side—comes from one of the Seventeenth Century families who have always run what we call Kuwait. He's not part of the great Al Shabah family, but no mere Customs official would dare give any trouble to guests on his airplane."

The tour bus came to a stop near the McLearys' hotel. They were headed for the Reception desk to cancel and pay for their room when Herb was detained by a uniformed chauffeur.

Herb spoke briefly to the chauffeur, returning highly agitated to relay news to Dennis. "Shucks, but Uncle's making me look a fool. He's sent this man to say he needs his plane tonight. If I want to go with him to collect his new boat, I need to be driven to the airport right away. Have you got your passport on you? Has Myriam any clothes she wants to bring? Toiletries? She'll have to collect them NOW."

Myriam didn't delay. She sped to their ground floor bedroom, packed her new dresses in a pillowcase, and was back at the Reception desk with Dennis's ever-ready duffle bag before Dennis had finished paying their bill.

From a cool Brooklyn street-wise pal, Herb became transformed into a nervous wreck, worrying he might miss the plane.

Myriam found she had to take skips to keep up with Herb, who didn't have longer legs than Dennis's, but seemed to gallop as fast as a Kentucky Derby winner she'd watched on the TransLux Theater's screen.

Feeling breathless, Myriam discovered that it wasn't easy to run with a four-month pregnancy; particularly when this pregnancy meant so much to her.

His Uncle's plane was waiting for Herb, its propellers whirling encouragingly.

There were two pilots, but only one other passenger, an elderly Kuwaiti in a navy business suit with a locked chain leading from his wrist to a square black box half a yard wide.

"Hi, Uncle," Herb sank into Arabic, while Myriam and Dennis used the miniscule bathroom to change into better clothes. Dennis relinquished his T-shirt and jeans for the navy blue suit he'd worn on Mehmet's wedding day. It was crushed and wrinkled from the duffle bag, but he reveled in the feel of it. Myriam squeezed into the largest of her three new dresses, wondering if the zipper would close on her favorite: a yellow chiffon more suitable for a tea dance than for travel in a small plane.

Myriam whispered between their secretive kisses: "Dennis, do you think this plane is used by smugglers to smuggle whiskey?"

"Sweetheart, I didn't see any crates on board."

"What do you reckon is in the Uncle's big square box?"

"Maybe diamonds?"

She didn't want any part in a smuggling scheme. She couldn't afford to be stopped by police: news of anything criminal would get fast as lightning to her father. "Dennis, do you think my father knows by now we've left Saudi Arabia?"

"He knows, thanks to Mehmet, that I left. Yes, and he'll have DESTINY's ex-owner for help in tracing my present whereabout. I only hope that Little Mother and Pop are safe enough in their camp now."

Myriam trembled, even though Dennis was using his body to shield her like an ancient knight's shimmering armor. She said: "My instinct told me we'd better leave that Kuwait City hotel. I felt it was the sort of place that sells valued information regarding its hotel's guests: their passport numbers, and—"

"You can say that again. Listen, this Herb is a big blabber-mouth. He could tell you what you want to know about his uncle's black box."

Myriam decided to take Dennis's advice. She tackled Herb directly.

He was seated in one of a pair of seats, reading ESQUIRE MAGAZINE, which he put down when Myriam took the companion seat.

Herb knew what she was going to ask.

He'd put off introducing the McLearys to Uncle until they'd change out of their grimy clothes. Another consideration that came to him was the possibility they could say something that could lower Uncle's opinion of him. He wanted to build on its present stature, not open it up to harmful comments.

"Herb, will you tell us what's in your uncle's long black box?"

"Shit, that? It's full of cash. High denomination bills."

"Money! But why doesn't he just put it in a bank?"

"He will. That's the point of this trip. He'll put it in a bank that pays interest. You see, devout Muslims are not allowed to charge interest on their money. So, they smuggle it out of the country to where they get interest. And after they get enough, they smuggle it back in. Don't worry: it's perfectly legal. I don't want to go to jail again." He returned to reading the magazine.

Myriam felt a bout of nausea coming on. She leaned over the top of the seat where Dennis was sitting.

She groaned: "I thought crossing the desert in a plane would be better than in a jeep. I was wrong. I think I'll have to make a run for the bathroom."

"Sweetheart, stay where you are. Use the paper bag to barf. This plane isn't acting normal. We're taking evasive action."

Herb agreed. "Got that right. We may have to ditch. Those guys are the air's pirates cohorts, after us."

Myriam, weakly, feeling yet another surge of nausea, asked: "Pirates? How's that possible?"

"They know when Uncle's transporting money. They circle above us until there are no other planes around. But we have the advantage: Uncle's prepared for this type of eventuality. He has a boat waiting near a beach where this plane can land. The air pirates' plane's too big for that stretch of beach."

Myriam opened the barf bag, vomited, and felt better until shooting began.

One pilot, hit, gave over the plane's controls to his co-pilot. He went into a nose dive, corrected, and made it to the right beach.

Herb had a comment for every scene. "This is a Cessna 172, damn good plane. And well maintained by the oil company Uncle bought it from. Hold on tight, we'll be safe."

Dennis unbuckled his safety belt, and—while the co-pilot completed the landing, Dennis applied a tourniquet to the pilot's heavily bleeding arm. "This man is going to need serious medical attention," he stated, never easing on the tourniquet.

Myriam, although her knees felt like jelly, scrambled to be first out of the plane. Following her came Herb's uncle, and Herb. Dennis stayed back with the wounded pilot, while reminding the co-pilot to pocket the flight plan.

Herb yelled at Dennis. "Idiot! You can't delay us. Our boat's bigger than the air pirates cohorts' boat but they can catch up to us on the water. Every second counts."

Dennis yelled back. "We can't just leave a wounded man."

"You're coming right now. Or we'll leave you behind. My uncle has people who know what can happen. My uncle makes provisions: his pilots will be all right. The wounded guy will get the best care."

They heard a motorboat approaching. Myriam sized it up, and felt relieved, judging it to be seaworthy. Quickly, Myriam dragged herself back to the stricken plane. She saw that the injured pilot was sitting up and drinking from a flask. "Dennis, please come. I'm sure you mean well, but we've got our baby to consider."

Dennis's face lit. He left the plane's bullet-ridden cockpit and went with Myriam to the beach to help Myriam go aboard the boat. That involved walking up to his knees in the water to lift her into a dinghy, then help her reach a makeshift gangway.

Once on board, a stewardess offered mint tea.

Herb complained. "Uncle, after that little gig, I think whiskey is in order. The hell with tea!" He'd rescued his copy of "ESQUIRE," and strolled into the cabin to sit down and read.

In the next hour the stewardess returned twice with more tea, accompanying that with egg sandwiches. Myriam managed to go to sleep on a sofa, while Herb continued reading 'ESQUIRE.'

Uncle was on his fourth cup of tea when the officer captaining the boat disturbed him.

"Sir, please excuse me, but we may have a problem. There is a catamaran that constantly tries to ram us. I have managed to out-race it. But now we are nearing the Strait of Hormuz."

"The Strait has a width of twenty-one nautical miles. Surely you can out-run this other vessel."

"Sir, we cannot race in the Strait of Hormuz. Should we be sunk, that could add to a pile-up that could block the transportation of oil from four countries."

"Here, my good man, smoke a cigar. Worry makes a man grow older."

"Sir, it is my solemn duty to advise you we must go to port at once."

"Captain, and I advise you that you are relieved of your duties." Uncle's voice dropped to a deep bass. "Herb, leave that filthy magazine and show this coward-of-a-captain why I paid for you to join the NEWTOWN Yacht Club."

An immediate change altered Herb's laconic style. He tossed "PLAYBOY" into a wastebasket and rushed from the cabin to the boat's wheel.

The boat changed from an elephant besieged by tigers to a seaborne missile.

Herb, who proved himself to be a star yachtsman, kept at his skill until safely beyond the Strait of Hormuz, where the aquatic tigers would not follow.

Hours later, Herb, still in his open neck shirt and casual slacks, brought Uncle's vessel to dock on Musandam, an enclave belonging to the Sultan of Oman. There was a space available in its Dibba port, and Herb gently eased the yacht to safety beside it.

The port of Dibba nestles below Musaldam's two thousand feet high mountain, which provides naturally cooled air to tourists from as far distant hot spots as Jerusalem. Cliffs and fjord-like waterways are other attractions to explore, but Dennis and Myriam preferred to be given a room at the best of Dibba's hotels, there to engage in the glories of their lovemaking.

Hours later, having showered, Dennis and Myriam relaxed sitting on the hotel's terrace overlooking the harbor.

Herb, basking in his new found role of hero, took on the challenge of attacking their afterglow with the banality of conversation. "I'm glad we saw as much as we did of

Kuwait. My third time to try to get to do Hajj, but my honesty won't let me be a hypocrite: I know I'll be back chasing girls as soon as I finish the prayers of repentance. Hell, I think I'd have liked to take my three turns around the Black Stone, throwing my pebbles in the traditional way. No, that's a lie. The truth is, I'm wondering right now how I can find a clean woman here in Dibba?"

Dennis, who hated losing his afterglow—a downer like watching the red ball of sun dive below the horizon—said: "Don't ask me to pimp for you. I've… Wait a minute! Do you see what I see? That ship… The one coming into the harbor. It's the DEVERON!"

Ecstatically, Myriam murmured: "Could we go see the captain who married us?"

Shrewd, narrow-eyed Uncle, although nearly asleep in a wicker rocking chair, grasped the importance to him of this news. He stood up from his chair and peered beyond the terrace to the filling harbor. Two cruise ships were crowding the DEVERON.

Chortling in a way that sounded like a noise from a broken harmonica, he said: "We ought to get out of Dibba before the pirates locate me. I can't load my black box on a rowboat to get out of here… But a British freighter?"

Herb, who had changed his slacks for a business suit, caught the urgency. He said: "I'm game. Listen Uncle, I'll go with my pals and find out if we can get passage to England." He summoned two rickshaws, and gave his order in Arabic.

By the time they reached DEVERON's dock, it was offloading food stuffs and onloading a cargo of limestone.

The ship was in busy mode. Herb, restless, wanted to give up and leave, with the idea of trying again later, but Dennis insisted he persevere. The threesome took a gangway to a lower deck.

Only minutes later Myriam saw Captain Igleton on a lower deck.

She sang out a huge "CAPTAIN, MY CAPTAIN."

That call drew his attention. Like a magnet draws a ring: he peered to their deck and bellowed a welcome. "My wedding kids! Here, in Dibba!" He took a quick glance at Myriam's bulge, and added: "I see that the wedding is bearing fruit. Anything more I can do for you?"

Dennis grabbed the moment.

He rushed to where the captain was overseeing the offloading from the other deck, a lower deck.

With great respect in his manner towards his former boss, Dennis asked: "Captain, is there any chance of passage out of Dibba for my friend Herb, here, who has literally just saved our lives?"

"Let me think." Herb and Myriam joined Dennis, to stand in front of the captain. A long nerve-wracking pause followed. Finally, after sweat was running down Herb's cheeks, Captain Igleton pressed the forefinger of his right hand with his thumb, and stated with little humor: "Two cabins come available in about an hour. I learned today we are losing a family of four. But these are my most expensive—"

Herb interrupted. With his Brooklyn manners, he said: "I have the proverbial rich uncle. He'll pay, whatever the cost. He'll want to sail with you too. And also pay for Dennis and Myriam. He'll pay anything, for the four of us."

Although he could have felt insulted by the inference of a bribe, Captain Igleton smiled kindly, unwilling to have this reunion spoiled: "On my ship, the cost will be the standard cost. No bribes accepted. See the Purser. He will explain this is our last port of call before Southampton. We can catch up tonight, at dinner."

Herb hastily found the Purser, and—as usual—using Uncle's spare credit card, paid for both cabins.

Dennis protested: "Herb, I'm totally broke. I can't repay your uncle. Ask the Purser to refund our two passages. I'll try—"

Herb interrupted. "And Uncle can't ever repay you for your help."

Their tickets in hand, the three returned to the hotel. Herb handed over the receipt for the credit card expense. Uncle swallowed, relieved, and patted Herb's back. Herb felt that showed he'd done enough good deeds, and headed for a whiskey taking Dennis with him. Meanwhile, Uncle aimed for the nearest ladies wear shop—his black box on the seat of a borrowed wheelchair—and treated Myriam to a complete trousseau.

Well before sailing time, the four were in their respective cabins. Myriam purred, touching the floor: "Dearest, do you remember our wedding night in a stateroom like this"

"Do I remember! But now that you're expecting our baby, we should use the double bed!"

When the ship was underway, Myriam decided to visit DEVERON's infirmary. "I haven't had a check-up, as you know." She said to Dennis. He accompanied her, but not without second thoughts. His last visit had been fraught with anxiety that he could have contracted tuberculosis from his bunk.

It was all smiles from the ship's doctor. He took Myriam's temperature, her blood pressure, and listened to her heart. "Baby is fine in there. But you, young mother-to-be, are much in need of good nourishment." He turned to wink at the expectant father, "And you, Dennis, could be her waiter!"

That wasn't a snide remark, and Dennis didn't take offense. He'd already worked out that it would be uncomfortable to be seated at the Captain's Table, after having jumped ship as a mere waiter. He didn't want to embarrass his former colleagues below stairs, he didn't want to embarrass the captain, or Myriam.

Leaving the infirmary, he opted to remain in their cabin with Myriam for all meals, until a week later when a severe storm broke out on their last night aboard. Myriam became seasick, and she left Dennis—who felt pressured to remain in their cabin—to find a lounge where there could be a cross current of fresh air. Myriam discovered that she wasn't alone in choosing the lounge. A grey-haired lady, attempting to read through her bifocals, swayed in her chair in tempo with the tossing ship. Nevertheless, the lady—obviously fighting seasickness—introduced herself. "I'm Sally Forrest. What's your name, dear? Don't try to speak, if you'd rather not."

"I'm Myriam McLeary. I've never seen it, but I believe that the name on my husband's passport says McLeary. As to why I came to a public room: the air up here in this lounge is better than in my cabin."

"I haven't seen you at dinnertime aboard any night. You are having a difficult pregnancy? I see you've 'joined the club.'"

"Yes, I'm almost four months pregnant. My husband and I preferred the quiet in our cabin. Will you allow me to call you Sally? And you'll call me Myriam."

"My pleasure. Are you traveling to visit relations in England?"

Myriam hesitated before replying. She didn't want to open her 'Pandora's Box.' Any mention of Mommy or her father led to minefields. She bit her lip, that permanent habit of hers when Myriam felt unresolved. After a long moment, she whispered: "No. And we don't know anyone in England.

We met two friends in Kuwait, who are on this ship: but they won't be staying in England for long. Perhaps you noticed a young American-type Muslim escorting his elderly Muslim uncle. They are my only friends."

"I CERTAINLY DID. It was heartening to watch the young man, who's so attentive to such an elderly person. Will you be seeing much of those two in England?"

"Afraid not. They'll be separating once the uncle has attended to business. I suppose you noticed the BLACK BOX CHAINED TO A WRIST? Once he's got rid of that he intends to return to Kuwait, while his nephew flies back to Brooklyn to be with his American father there. I'll miss them."

"Surely you'll find new ones in England."

"If I do, they won't be Muslims. I don't belong to their Muslim faith any more. I appreciate the uncle's generosity and the nephew's bravery, but I have reason to fear Muslim cruelty. I can't accept how Muslims permit beheadings. Right now, I'm looking for a faith I could join. I haven't decided on one yet."

"I'm a member of the Religious Society of Friends. We don't look to have people join us. We are happy in our belief in the Inner Light: that is the direct awareness of God. It allows a person to know God. It may not ring a bell with you. But you may have heard of our work: we try to help people in need."

"Quakers, helping people in need! I'm on this ship, thanks to a Quaker lady giving me her passport. Maybe you know her: Beryl Waites. She distributes food from welcome trolleys in an oil camp in Kuwait."

"Dear Beryl, I know her well. We belong to the same Meeting House on Euston Road in northwest London. You want to know more Beryls? Come to our First Day meeting. I'll be there, I'll introduce you to women of her age and to some of your own. We have an expectant mothers group; those girls will help you to find everything you'll need for your baby: doctor, hospital, diapers, bassinet. They come to Euston Road house every Thursday at eleven. But you'll have to excuse me for now: I have to run to the nearest Ladies Room." Clutching a not-so-clean handkerchief to her tightened mouth, Sally disappeared into a bathroom to lose her lunch.

Chapter 11

London, England

With the DEVERON approaching Southampton, where they were going to enter England as refugees using Dennis's passport, Dennis and Myriam peered happily from their cabin's porthole at the RMS Queen Mary, leaving her western dock.

The DEVERON had dockage in a less elegant area, but Uncle had wired ahead for a Rolls Royce to be present to whisk the four ex-passengers to London. In the car, he asked: "Dennis, do you have any more good ideas for me? I need the name of a respectable bank, that will pay interest on the contents of my black box."

Myriam, lightheaded in her joyful mood, almost ruined Dennis's reply, wanting to inquire if Uncle slept with the box's chain locked to his wrist.

Fortunately, she kept quiet out of gratitude for his paying their passages.

Dennis replied, in an equally serious tone: "You know my background. That I've been in prison. But it was for fornicating with a fourteen-year-old girl, not for robbery. I don't want to recommend any banks. I've never been to London. Deedee Murray Pierce always sent my money through National City. That is, until the next-to-final payout in Kuwait, where she wired it through a Coutts Bank. You could have Herb use his U.S. Consulate to find out about the reputation of Coutts."

An hour later, after settling at Claridge's Hotel on Brook Street, Uncle left its sedate lobby in another Rolls Royce.

With a letter recommending Coutts as one of London's most esteemed long-lived banks, Uncle drove to his final destination with the black box's chain still locked to his wrist. At Coutts branch bank near Piccadilly, after Uncle had finally unlocked its chain, the black box was placed in a convenient trolley to move its contents to the Manager's office.

Chapter 12

Open Sea, The English Channel

Uncle swept majestically up to the Manager.

Following courteous introductions, he said: "I have studied your rate of interest on certain bonds. I will tell you I have brought a considerable amount to invest. It is from extracting oil in Kuwait; I have the names of the investors, all highly respectable."

Before papers were signed, canny old Uncle asked a favor. He chose his words carefully.

"There is a young American named Dennis McLeary, who recently did me a great favor when I needed passage on a ship where he had worked previously. He needs employment. His Saudi wife is expecting a child: they know no one in Great Britain. He has a letter of recommendation from the captain of that ship—a very honorable man I now know personally—who married the pair. Incidentally, his wife has an illustrious Saudi heritage. Unfortunately Dennis, he served seventeen years in a Florida prison for intercourse with a fourteen-year-old girl. He has paid his debt to society. Could you find a job for him at Coutts?"

A long, heavy silence followed.

Uncle was habituated to long heavy silences during a deal.

He waited tolerantly after the Manager debated with an employee who had been summoned.

Following much whispering between them, the Manager nodded his head in agreement toward Uncle and instructed his employee to give him his calling card, with the understanding that Dennis McLeary could have a job interview that afternoon.

The business ended with more formal courtesy.

Back at Claridge's, Uncle passed the card and good news to Dennis, who had readied his duffle-bag to move to a less expensive hotel. "Sorry, Uncle, that my wife isn't here to thank you and say a temporary goodbye. She left that to me."

"Any of our goodbyes must be temporary."

"Myriam has gone to a local Quaker Meeting House, while I look for affordable rooms that will include one for our coming baby. But tomorrow night I hope I can afford to give a dinner for you and Herb."

"We'll keep the date open, Dennis."

"Myriam's exact words were: 'I know you won't give Herb's Uncle a kiss from me, but you can tell him I've gone to meet with a group of expectant mothers at a Quaker

Meeting House. I'm hoping to learn about my Inner Light'."

When Dennis and Myriam were reunited in the furnished two-up two-down cottage he'd found, Myriam filled him in on her experience at the Meeting House on Euston Road.

"Wonder upon wonder, as my mother used to say! I've made at least six friends; I've already bought diapers and a snowsuit at a discount baby store they took me to. And wait until I tell you about the Inner Light. I had a most idyllic moment inside the Meeting House. I must take you there in two days so you can find your Inner Light."

"Hold on: diapers with another five months to wait for our baby's arrival? And a snowsuit in September? But, my darling, do pass on to me your idyllic moment. Up to now, all the ones I've ever had have been with you."

The next morning, while Dennis was at his new job, a bus took Myriam to the Euston Road Meeting House. Inside, she found a chair in the main room. A Meeting was in progress.

A Quaker woman, wearing eyeglasses that kept sliding down her nose, read a translation of a poem by Boris Pasternak, Soviet Russia's greatest poet, whose works had to be smuggled out to the West. The poem's subject was love:

During the long silence that followed, Myriam began to have a series of pleasant shakes. An extraordinary peace enveloped her: she'd found her Inner Light.

On her bus all the way home, Myriam retained her aura of joy.

Dennis was waiting at their front door. Looking past Myriam to evade her eyes, he listened to a cuckoo bird calling from Epping Forest. "You've made us late for dinner," he grunted. Then, seeing her radiant face, he took her in his arms, before adding: "We can take a cab to Claridge's. I realize you have something important to tell me."

"Yes, I have. But dear, we'll take the bus. Uncle and Herb will be glad to have waited when I tell them what happened." In the bus, there were no empty seats. Myriam had to delay her news as she swayed from side to side holding on to a ceiling strap. Nobody had noticed that she was pregnant, until one man stood up and offered her his place. She thanked him, but made space for Dennis to squeeze in next to her.

"My darling: I found my Inner Light," she breathed ecstatically.

"Myriam! But that's great! I know how much that will mean to you. But, on another tack, I want to tell you that I've invited a young lady to join our dinner party."

Playing at being offended, Myriam groaned: "Do I look so awful, being pregnant, that you are starting to look for other women?"

Dennis laughed, lovingly, causing street-goers to turn and stare down their sniffing noses. "My precious, brilliant wife, no one will ever be able to compete with you under any circumstances. But I met at the bank a Muslim woman who deals with our Muslim clients. Her name is Aida Eldesouky; she's Egyptian and I thought she'd be a great pal for you, my darling."

At Claridge's, on hearing of the addition of a young Muslim woman to the dinner party, Uncle immediately caught the nuances that hung like icicles beside an open window. Once ensconced inside the leased Rolls Royce, he used the short drive to Wheeler's to evolve a plot that could benefit Herb's tarnished soul. He'd already postponed his return to Kuwait. Now he determined to remain in London until some miracle could alter Herb's erotic way of life.

Leaving the car to enter the restaurant, Uncle resolved to spend as much effort—

and money—for the miracle as would be necessary.

While Wheelers' Maitre D. seated the party at a table already occupied by a twenty-ish good looking brunette woman, Uncle used his courteous old-fashioned charm to salute her in his most amiable manner, using a high grade of the Arabic language.

He introduced himself and his nephew, "Call me Uncle, please. I call my nephew by his correct name: Halo, but, everyone else calls him Herb," and then gave the podium to Dennis, who introduced Myriam in English.

Herb, like a bulldozer crushing a field of daisies, plowed ahead with a flip advertisement of his manner of treating street women he could buy. "Hi, we can skip this boring dinner to find a suite in a fun hotel."

Although appalled at Herb's behavior towards a girl he knew to be an employee at Coutts, Uncle said nothing. He wanted to wait and measure Aida by the way in which she reacted.

Dennis, who felt bruised by the word "boring" to describe his attempt to repay Uncle's generosity, also said nothing. His instinct warned him to follow Uncle's lead.

Aida, smiling as if she recalled a line of dialogue from a well-known play, said slowly: "How interesting that you're quoting Noel Coward. His critics complain that his work no longer appeals to a young generation. Personally, I like the famous line when his heroine strides across the stage muttering something like, "My lipstick... I must have my lipstick." To underscore, Aida opened her handbag, held high a lipstick, and proceeded to refresh her lips' color.

Touchdown.

Myriam rushed in to change the subject. "Do you ever go to auctions? I would love to have a friend to go with me. I don't really need anything—our cottage came so completely furnished—but I read in the TIMES that many of the great landowners are divesting themselves of antiques—like sheep shorn for slaughter—now that great houses are being replaced by high-rises."

"I'd love to go antiquing with you. I'm free on weekends. " Aida's hazel eyes danced at the prospect of visiting Sotheby's and Christie's. As with many other famous venues, Aida had missed out by conforming to most Muslim rules for women on their own, adhering to those rules even when in a country where the majority were Christians. "I've missed out on a lot by never going out alone."

Uncle pleased at this hint that she was a devout Muslim, asked: "Mademoiselle Aida, could you suggest a Mosque near here for Friday prayers, that Halo and I could go to?"

"Yes. There's one only a few streets away. I'll show you the way."

After giving his entrée order to a hovering waiter, "Dover Sole, with brown rice," Uncle said to Dennis: "Let us leave the ladies while they talk antiques. Come to the washroom."

Dennis complied, although he still felt endangered when going into a washroom with another man.

Inside the nearest Men's Room, while both soaped their hands, Uncle unburdened himself. "Dennis, you have often told me you want to repay my favors. You can do that now. I need help in the next few days to redeem my nephew. Also, I must stop him from this lack of respect for Allah. Halo says he needs a woman every day. Fine, if he is married to her. I must find a suitable wife for Halo. I guessed you were matchmaking when you brought Aida to dinner. Halo certainly liked her, but in the wrong way. Together we must find him a wife. Let us return to the table and make some suggestions."

Back at the table, Uncle began his ploy by asking: "How would you like to go sailing off East Brighton on Saturday?".

With his usual lack of grace, Herb interrupted: "I'm going horseracing at Ascot, Saturday."

Dennis agreed quickly. "Great. We'll all go to Ascot for the races. Aida, how about it? Will you join us? And, Uncle, you'd like that! You'd come too."

Uncle nodded, tentatively, as if he was falling asleep. "Yes, I'll go and Mademoiselle Aida will enjoy herself because one of my investors owns a horse in one of Saturday's races and can get us good seats and lunch in a private box. But do not give up on East Brighton. Go there on Sunday."

"Done deal. I'll buy a stunning hat for Ascot for Myriam, and then the swimsuits."

Grumbling, but looking sedated as if he'd been given a dose of laudanum, Herb put in: "My Newport Yacht Club has reciprocal rights to most sailing clubs. I could rent a sailboat."

Aida's voice floated like a summer cloud over edelweiss: "I'm not much of a swimmer, but I love sailing. Yes, please. Let's plan on East Brighton for Sunday."

Grudgingly, Herb agreed, but kept his personal options open by making a condition: "That's if I'm not included in something else more exciting."

His graceless condition tainted the plans, placing them second rate.

Aida trumped that comment as she had earlier ones: smiling widely make it know that she was enthralled with the idea of an afternoon at Ascot Races and a day of summer sailing.

Uncle's first ploy worked well. His leased Rolls Royce collected Aida early Friday morning to drive the three Muslims to her Mosque. No same sex problem there. Aida disappeared upstairs to be isolated with other devout women. She was the only one wearing a slacks suit: most of the ladies had obviously been raiding Harrod's Women's Wear for dresses.

When prayers were over, Uncle stayed on to speak with an Iman, while sending Dennis and Aida in the Rolls Royce to their jobs at Coutts Bank.

Left alone in her Epping cottage, Myriam did house cleaning until tossing down her dust-rag and heading for the nearest tube station to take the underground to Peter Jones Department Store. Under her breath, she'd said: "I can buy my own hat for Ascot."

In the hat department she was attended by a strong-willed saleswoman. "You don't want any of wide-brimmed fanciful chapeaus. This is not June, and the races tomorrow are not the Royal Ascot Races." The officious, middle-aged woman reproved Myriam, holding out to her a town hat with a narrow brim.

Myriam left the saleswoman to cross the millinery department to where a mannequin was placed. The plaster mannequin had red hair the same carrot shade as Myriam's, topped by a felt bowler in blue over a printed dress... Myriam stood high on her toes, reached the bowler, and paid for it at the nearest cashier. Uncle's purchases for her in Dibba had included a silk suit in that same blue.

She asked the cashier: "Could you point me toward the section for swimsuits?"

"Certainly, Madame. Go straight to the back of this floor. Its' a little late for the summer swimming season, but you might find some on sale there."

Myriam hurried to the floor's far end, and selected a number suitable for a four months mother-to-be. She found the Men's Section, and chose a pair of trunks fashionably designed to reach Dennis's knees.

Saturday morning dawned grey and forbidding. "I'll ruin my shoes in the mud if we walk around a lot at Ascot." Myriam said, reaching Dennis at Coutts' front door, where he was waiting for Uncle's leased Rolls Royce.

"You could take two pairs of shoes. Neither pair your best. Aida told me she always takes two pairs of stockings in case one gets a run."

"You've seen Aida?"

"Not since Friday. Met her in our corridor. She was so excited over the plans for Ascot and East Brighton."

"Any mention of Herb?

"None."

"I needed to speak to her, Darling. Uncle wants her to be fully aware that he has the money, not Herb."

"She's not a gold-digger."

"That's my opinion, too. I told Uncle that she's had plenty of opportunities to grab any one of those oil-rich Arab clients of Coutts. She hasn't."

The Rolls Royce drew up to the door. Dennis and Myriam ceased speaking about Aida. She was already inside and had taken one of the jump seats in order to leave plenty of space on the sofa-like seat in the back.

Dennis took the other jump seat. Uncle and Herb were crushed very close to Myriam. But the weather was cool and the long ride to Windsor went well.

Uncle was the one who talked to Aida.

"Tell me, Mademoiselle Aida, what you think of contangos. Several of the investors I deal with have asked me about them. With contangos it doesn't look like usury when you make money from them."

"Sir, I'm often asked about them. I tell investors not to touch them. I'd think more favorably of contangos if our world was a safer place. Here we are driving past so many buildings bombed by planes from World

War Two… Such devastation. But when the buildings were built in the turn of the century, there were no airplanes. No Wright brothers had taken one up. There were no buzz bombs to leave entire neighborhoods wiped out. And now we have nuclear! With contangos it is essential to accept the possibility of depravation. Downturn when you make an investment of say $100, expecting it to go to $109 and to sell it with a nine percent profit, you may find that the investment went to $89, and you lost $11. Not for my investors!"

Dennis watched Uncle, and recognized the same gleam in his eyes that had been there in Dibba when DEVERON appeared.

Aida's Ascot hat was a discreet felt one with a waving brim that somehow produced a lilt to its style. With the Rolls Royce slowing into Ascot's Main Street, she secured her hat firmly with two hatpins.

The Rolls Royce, readied with an owner's sticker, entered the lot marked Owners and Trainers, opposite the Main Entrance .

Myriam said: "Look over there, at the car opposite."

The auto was a large Daimler, with the royal emblem heralding its importance over the front grill.

When Uncle showed their tickets to enter the line of private boxes, Dennis saw King George VI, his Queen Elizabeth and their daughters Princess Elizabeth and Princess Margaret Rose mounting steps leading to their private box. He pressed Myriam's arm, making sure she would not miss this vignette.

The afternoon seemed to get better. Uncle's investor invited the five from the Rolls Royce to go into the ante paddock to watch his horse being saddled. When they proceeded from their high stools of the ante paddock to the main paddock and headed for a tree for shade, they were courteously but firmly sidelined by an Ascot employee wearing the royal employees' crested hat and green velvet coat.

King George VI and his Queen Elizabeth came strolling through a parting crowd of on-lookers and took a stance under the tree Dennis had selected. Their Majesties' horse trainer joined them, and opened his racing program to make a point to the Queen.

There followed another moment of excitement as this race's jockeys entered the paddock.

Queen Elizabeth, who was listed as owning a horse in the race, spoke at length to her jockey until he mounted his contender and galloped down the racecourse to the Starting Line.

Immediately, Their Majesties left the paddock to view the race from their box.

The entire crowd in the paddock followed, many racegoers pushing others to guarantee a better viewing position on the grass near the Finish Line.

Aida, standing at the front rail of the investor's box, said: "Look! So many men are taking off their hats, expecting the Queen's horse to win. They'll throw them in the air if that happens."

Although in a prime place to view it, Aida missed the Off from the Starting Gate because she'd turned to say a word to Herb: "Great!"

Soon the competing horses spread out unevenly on the back stretch, some horses being held back for a later championship-style run. The Queen's horse raced mid-field, with the investor's not far behind.

A tremendous noise erupted: it came from the throats of thousands of viewers present. But it wasn't due to a win. The competing horses were still spread out unevenly in the back stretch only beginning to accelerate as they prepared for their final run. The noise, still growing greater, was induced because a jockey had tumbled from his fallen horse, and both the horse and jockey lay—unmoving—on the trampled grass.

Dennis and Myriam joined Aida at the front of the investor's box. Myriam covered her eyes: "I can't look."

Shuddering, Aida borrowed a pair of binoculars. "The jockey is raising his head, but his horse hasn't been able to stand up."

While the competing horses accelerated down the final stretch, a green curtain was erected to mask the agonies of the dying horse hundreds of yards distant. A stretcher was duly brought to collect the injured jockey, precisely at the very moment the winner took the race.

The Queen's horse hadn't placed. Instead of standing next to the First, or Second or Third post to pat her horse, the Queen was busily writing a note. This she handed to an equerry.

Myriam commented, as the equerry handed the note to the dead horse's grieving owner: "What a great racing lady Queen Elizabeth is."

Behind, holding a half-full glass of whiskey, Herb complained: "I had a bet on the Second. My bet was 30-1. I could have cleaned up if that damned fool jockey hadn't fallen down and hadn't brought on all that disruptive noise."

Uncle came up to the box's railing to interrupt Herb. "The Queen and the King will be going to have tea in the rear of their box. My investor is inviting us to tea in the Jockey Club Rooms of Newmarket's section"

With Herb possessively attached to his half-glass of whiskey, the group trailed down one flight of stairs and up the stands for tea.

In the Jockey Club's area were the main owners of horse-breeding estates. Sad whispers and the shaking of heads were rife in this stand, as owners commiserated with one another about the horrific scene below

The scene grew worse. The dead horse's owner was seen to climb into the van containing her dead horse and then proceed to hug his carcass while kissing its head.

The Jockey Club section overlooked the royal box. The two royal princesses hadn't left with their parents for tea. They'd remained watching the owner bemoaning the cruel death of her contender. Princess Margaret Rose wiped tears of sympathy, while Princess Elizabeth, a fairly recent bride, placed an arm around her sister.

Teatime over, Uncle decided that his group should avoid the five o'clock traffic and head for London. He kissed his host on both cheeks, thanked him for the race day, and packed the other four members of the party into the leased Rolls Royce. This time he made certain that Myriam took a jump seat, and Herb was squeezed next to Aida for the long ride to their individual homes.

Sunday morning, Myriam led Dennis to the early Meeting on Euston Road. "Quakers call this First Day, and we'll be among the first to arrive on First Day." Inside she immediately met with two of the expectant mothers from Thursday's group.

The women solemnly chose seats near where the four stands of chairs met. Myriam and Dennis followed them. They took front row seats.

Soft silence.

A longer silence.

Dennis's hands began to shake. He took one of Myriam's hands in his. Hers were shaking too.

Half an hour passed. A member of the Meeting stood up and read from the Muslim Koran "O You who believe! Enter absolutely into peace." He added nothing and sat down.

When the full hour of the Meeting ended, Myriam's was hugged by the two expectant mothers, and then she joined Dennis for the nearest bus stop.

Seated on their way to meet Herb at Claridge's, Dennis made a hopeful comment like the first song of a bird at dawn. "I certainly would like to believe. And God knows I want peace. But how extraordinary that the Koran should be quoted in a Quaker Meeting."

"I think it's wonderful." Myriam's smile was radiant. "I can't put into words how happy this has made me, helping me to grow my Inner Light. Dennis, did you find yours?"

"I hope that's true. Hoping you're half way there. Listen darling, you're a fantastic swimmer, but you didn't do the Australian crawl without learning to paddle."

"Not today. Maybe later. Give me time."

All the time in the world.

"I certainly believe in having an Inner Light". "I'm not sure I'm clean enough for it."

"Dennis! Of course you are. Except for squalling on the prison's chaplain , I don't know of any awful thing. And anyway, God loves to forgive sinners."

When they arrived at their cottage, Dennis was still resisting Myriam's suggestions.

Dennis ended the debate by grabbing the bag of swimsuits and changing the subject.

"Let me carry the bag of swimsuits. You're going to have a long day."

"I won't"

"Be careful what you predict. The bad elves might hear and turn things around."

They were laughing together, when they caught sight of Herb and Aida park outside Claridges already seated in a red jaguar with its top down. "Don't worry about getting a ticket. Or should I say 'summons'. The doorman just told me that ones morning a lady member of a Hunt brought her horse to the front entrance of Claridge's and handed him her reins while she went inside for coffee."

All four laughed together riding down Oxford Street, while Herb—although bowling along over the city speed limit—managed to find the route to East Brighton.

Herb was in an exceptionally good mood. "This Jag sure beats the pathetic bus in Kuwait that took you, me and Myriam into the city from that woeful display of Greek ruins. This red baby can make speeds over 130 miles an hour."

Aida agreed, "Terrific car. I don't know if we'll be on a road that allows the Jag to show off its awesome speed, but we'll see plenty of wonders today besides this wonderful car."

Myriam said: "Tell us. Give us an example."

Herb grabbed the conversation: "I told the Concierge that I wanted to know what's the best way to get the most out of East Brighton. He's a racing fan, so he said we should go to the horseraces there tomorrow. When I explained we'd spent yesterday at inimitable Ascot, he suggested the Prince's Pavillion. Actually, he called it "Prinny's Brothel."

Surprising Myriam, Aida sang out: "One of the most gorgeous examples of John Nash architecture you could dream of. I've never been to the East Brighton Pavillion. But I've seen plenty of postcards of it sent to me by Coutts' customers."

Herb brought the red Jaguar convertible with public parking space for the Prince's Pavillion to as much accuracy as a seagull diving to catch a live hermit crab emerging from a conch shell.

The foursome had a perfect view of Prinny's Folly. John Nash's architectural genius added a particular splendor to the grouping of onion-shaped Russian style roofs and Indian arches. There were Christian crosses topping five of these roofs. On either side of the grandest and largest of the onion-shaped roofs stood four towers that could serve Muezzins calling for praise of Allah.

Inside, the main rooms were either suitable for an English country-gentlemen, or a pasha from East of the Red Sea.

Aida commented: "That one mantelpiece could fit any fine estate, but the rooms for a seraglio, they're something else. I became interested in the story of the Prince Regent because he commissioned Nash to build this place. Unhappy in his marriage to a first cousin, he was having a series of love affairs. Probably the great love of his life was Lady Fitzherbert. But it was probably years after her time, that the Prince Regent took refuge here following the terrible tragedy that blighted his Regency."

"What tragedy?" Myriam asked, her hand on a fanciful doorknob.

"At the time, his mistress was Lady Hertford, and he was staying at her husband's estate when he learned that his daughter, Princess Charlotte heir to the throne, had gone into labor. He traveled back to Carlton House in London, to go to sleep while waiting for more news. When woken up to be told that Princess Charlotte had given birth to a still-born son, he felt sad to have lost a possible male heir to the throne: but not sad enough. He chose to go back to sleep, without asking any questions about Charlotte's condition."

"But you said a terrible tragedy."

"Yes. Meanwhile, after thirty hours of excruciating labor due to the baby being in transverse position, Princess Charlotte's pulse was failing. Her doctor, Sir Richard Croft, had not manually repositioned the fetus earlier and had allowed the princess to deliver a still-born child. No Cesarean.

No anesthetic, because chloroform hadn't been invented. Then he decided not to wait for her placenta to come out normally, but thrust his hands into her to grab it and pulled it out. Intense bleeding followed. She never complained or 'shrieked.' To alleviate her pain, Sir Richard gave her wine. Another no-no, because wine thins blood. Her husband's doctor, who was also present, heard her say: "They have made me tipsy.' Soon after she drew up her legs to her chin, finally complained of pain, and died. After being informed of her death, the Prince Regent went to see her body in her Surrey home, Claremont House, then traveled to East Brighton. There followed a public outcry: Sir Richard Croft committed suicide. The Prince Regent stayed in East Brighton too long."

Myriam, suffering through this story like a deer in a trap, groaned, "Too awful."

Herb, bored, snidely remarked: "Maybe he'd needed this type of architecture to get him hot."

Appropriately, a foggy atmosphere descended.

Aida's voice lost its lilt. "Princess Charlotte's death brought a sad blight on this place. When the Prince Regent became King George IV and had more architects create expensive additions, his popularity had faded. But today's war-weary tourists like the grandeur. So many great houses have disappeared in the bombings or were dismantled to save taxes."

Dennis, always poignantly aware of Myriam's pregnancy, swiftly changed the subject. Pointing to a fading sepia print dated 1915, he said: "This place became the Indian Hospital during the First World War. Very suitable architecture for that."

Herb broke in: "I'll need a hospital if we don't leave now. Boredom has me by the throat, and I'm choking."

He hurried the other three to the red Jaguar.

Finding the beach gave him the chance to locate the East Brighton Sailing Club. He parked the Jaguar in the club's parking lot and with an at-home swagger, led his group inside.

Herb, after a word with the Manager, got permission for his party to enjoy the club's Sunday buffet lunch. It featured local seafood, but there were traditional dishes too: Dennis chose the hot shepherd's pie, because the temperature had dropped and he'd begun to feel feverish from an oncoming cold.

Aida arranged to have a hefty picnic basket packed for them by the club's accommodating chef.

Herb, after learning that boats were not for hire at the Sailing Club, asked for a telephone, dialed Claridge's number, and spoke to Uncle. Within minutes Uncle had arranged for another of his investors to lend his yacht that was docked at the Sailing Club. While Herb showed his identification according to the description telephoned in by the investor-owner, Dennis and Myriam used the club's changing rooms to put on their bathing suits.

A club secretary showed Herb the way to locate the investor's sailboat, after providing all four with life vests.

With a hearty: "Good sailing," he left Herb to familiarize himself with the yacht.

A willing club member then offered to show the foursome how to operate the investor's sailboat. The member turned out to be overly talkative: "A beauty. Huge. You'd have no trouble handling her on your own in these waters, but you'll need a two-man crew if you go any distance."

Myriam, delighted with the boat, caroled: "Herb, she's lovely. Let this nice man show you how to sail her."

"I know all that I need to know."

The loquacious member pushed on: "I'll bet that you don't".

Herb, always having to feel superior, grumbled: "I've sailed on grander!"

"This info isn't regarding his yacht: it's about the owner. He has only been on it twice. Once a year since he commissioned it. He's a Muslim, located in some far distant Arab country, where he built up a reputation for being extremely devout. But when he travels to England, he hires a broad to spend a day with him on this boat. Total privacy! Get the picture? No ship-to-shore telephone or radio on board. He doesn't want to register at a public hotel.

Maybe afraid of being blackmailed later by the broad because he doesn't want to be branded an adulterer. Rather like the Prince Regent and his Pleasure Palace, wouldn't you say?"

Angrily, Herb growled: "Shut up! Scram! I want to get out to sea, not listen to stupid gossip."

The member's wide smile waned. He left Herb's party to join up with two members who had left their boat and were using extra lines to tie her to the dock. His fading voice could be heard warning his fellow members: "Heard on the club's radio that a terrific storm is heading our way. I guess you heard it too. I believe you were traveling West, right into its eye. The only good anyone could expect from this storm would be if its winds hurry along those yachts sailing to London."

Dennis heard his comments and led Myriam to the yacht's stern. "We'd better get into the water before that storm hits."

Herb dashed any hope of a swim as soon as he steered to open water. He said: "I'm going to see what this yacht's capable of." Within minutes, the sailboat had reached forty knots and was bracing against the now emerging storm. "She can do better than forty!" Herb yelled into the increasing wind.

When the wind reached sixty miles an hour, Herb called to Dennis: "Take the tiller, I'm going to raise the jib. I'll get this baby to make like one of Radio City's Rockettes, kick right over the waves."

Dennis poured all his vigor into controlling the obstinate tiller. He'd believed that Herb would race for a few miles, but it turned out that Herb raced East for half the night, always guiding the yacht according to the many shore lights.

He could hear Herb yelling excitedly, "Got it! Watch this baby—I'm going to smash world records!"

Herb, yelling, failed to see the sailboat's boom coming at him. It him hard, sweeping him into the waves.

Chapter 13

Mortuary

Myriam and Aida didn't hear the thud when the boom struck Herb. They didn't hear the splash when his body broke into the sea. Both were asleep; they'd taken a nap five hours into Herb's wild sailing. Myriam had changed back into her street clothes, Aida had added her sweater: those had kept them warm until they raced into the freezing rain on deck after the sound of Dennis shouting: "Herb, overboard! Aida, take the tiller: I'm going after him."

Aida didn't linger neither did Myriam both girl came to top-side, quick as two ponies, to follow orders. Aida took the tiller. Dennis, only waiting until he'd pressed her hands to the bucking wood, dove into the dark waves to locate Herb.

Splash! Silence from Dennis. Only the cruel wind and biting rain could be heard above the seas' roar.

With the moon waning, there was fatally little light.

Almost blinded by the salt spray, and impeded by the lack of a shimmer or glow on the spray, Dennis worked his way against the waves.

Herb!

Dennis glimpsed a form ahead. With one of his arms he hit flesh; his left hand caught a firm hold onto Herb's safety vest.

Herb, unconscious, had been found due to a reflection from the life vest's white cloth.

Dennis, struggling, managed to pull Herb's helpless body to reach the sailboat's side. There, Myriam helped to tug him on to the deck, with Dennis pushing from behind.

Aida shouted into the wind: "Dennis, take back the tiller. Myriam and I can get Herb into the bed in the cabin." She handed over the tiller, and the two girls carefully slid his body down the steps.

They were lifting Herb onto the bed, when Myriam said: "Look, Aida! Look at that bump on Herb's forehead!"

"I see it. He'll need medical help. Surgery, to operate on that ugly thing." Aida felt around the bump. "We must head for shore."

She left Herb, went top-side again and cornered Dennis. "Can you head for shore, or will the wind get into the top of the mainsail and topple us into the briny?"

"Don't know. The wind's in charge. The sailboat could tip over."

Together they heard Myriam calling: "Herb's conscious, but raving. One of you come quickly."

Dennis answered that call, leaving Aida again with the tiller. Herb, his sheet covered with blood, had opened his eyes. The lids were heavy.

Delirious, Herb didn't make any sense.

A bulb-sized knob on his head warned of a hematoma. "Good grief! "Myriam gasped. "We've got to get Herb to a hospital, fast. Blood could reach his brain!"

Kneeling, Dennis put both his arms around Herb, and hugged him.

Dennis hadn't hugged another male since he'd been an innocent six-year-old. "I'm here for you."

Dennis placed his head near Herb's lips. No longer delirious, Herb whispered: "Tell my parents… Sorry was such a brat… Tell Uncle… guessed his plan, but wanted choose wife myself… Next year, when I come to do Hajj—"

A death gurgle interrupted.

Herb died.

Dennis shut his lids, and covered Herb's head with the bloodied sheet. He said: "We'll head for shore. Too late for a hospital. Got to find an undertaker."

From the tiller, Aida shouted: "No! No hospital under any circumstances! Dennis, take back the tiller and I'll explain."

A change had overtaken Aida. From the acquiescent, always ready-to-please-Herb girl, Aida had mutated into a frenzied zealot.

Down in the cabin, aghast at Herb's death, Myriam began to weep. "I knew Herb better after he joined his uncle." "A realm of tears followed."

Dennis couldn't comfort her; he had this arrogant Aida to deal with at the tiller.

Aida repeated, saliva spitting. "No hospital."

Dennis heard her and took over the tiller without any comment.

Alone in the cabin with Myriam, Aida broached the subject in the same belligerent tone: "No Undertaker. That means police. Police can eventually mean an inquest, maybe a judge and jury. We aren't Herb's relations. We may even end up as defendants if there is an insurance claim from the yacht owner's insurance people. But most important, hear me, is that Herb—as a Muslim—must be washed, shrouded and buried within twenty-four hours of death."

She shouted loud enough for Dennis to be fully alerted.

Dennis hurled his comment from the tiller: "Know about that. Went to a Muslim funeral on DEVERON."

Back on deck, Myriam tried, gently and from friendship, to calm Aida. "Not possible to avoid the police. Herb's dead from an accident that must be reported."

Aida contradicted. "There is a way. We'll take Herb aboard this sailboat to London and give his body over to Uncle."

"To Uncle!"

"He met a friendly Iman at my mosque who deals with burials. He's the Iman who took on London's local Government over the problem of delaying burials because of such as Inquests. This Iman will send the mortuary people who will prepare Herb for his body wash and to be wrapped in a shroud. It is preferable that a relative be present. Voila, Uncle!

"And who is going to sail the boat to London?"

"I am. With help from Dennis."

Myriam interrupted fiercely: "My husband trained to be a chauffeur. He knows next to nothing about sailing."

Dennis called down: "Mr. Blunt took me on a smaller version of this boat to sail on Lake Okeechobee. I'm used to a tiller. I know about the twenty-four hour deadline for a Muslim to be buried. It was because a Muslim waiter died on the DEVERON that I got my chance to get out of New York before I'd have had to serve prison time again. I went to that man's funeral."

Myriam lost her belligerence. She bit her lip and wailed: "We're all going to drown."

"Not if we use common sense and share the responsibilities. Anyway, we're halfway there after Herb's phony race. Herb got us this far, and he deserves a proper Muslim burial." Aida's tone sounded like a drill sergeant's. "You, Myriam, must serve us the picnic I inveigled from the left-overs of the club buffet. I've had a nap, but I can't think without some nourishment. You, Dennis, I propose another hour at the tiller. I'll scan the horizon to keep us parallel to what's visible of the shoreline. For the time being, before I take over the tiller, that's going to be my job. That, and satisfying my curiosity as to England's famous southeast coast."

Dennis did his job: he familiarized himself with the ebb and flow of the shoreline's towns and the intervening high rises that signified a city.

The ship passed North Foreland: the haunt of weathermen.

Dennis shouted to it: "Don't you weathermen ever get a forecast right?" His yell was lost in the unpredicted wild wind.

Thames River's mouth arrived sooner than expected. Aida peered into its waters for any sign of the spawning salmon said to predict when the water would be clean enough for human consumption.

It had been graced by famous visitors such as Julius Caesar. He reached this area sixty years before the birth of Christ, and had described its waters as: "Wonderful."

But very recently the Nazi bombers in World War Two had used the Thames's mouth as a navigator's instrument to show the way to London. That fact defiled its reputation as a happy place.

With the palms of their hands sore and their fingers nearly paralyzed, Dennis and

Aida—while continuing to alternate duty at the tiller—derived some pleasure from a vignette alongside. Aida called to Myriam: "Look, we aren't the only sailboat limping toward London's docks. Two more, in fact. I spot one from the Channel Islands' Bailiwick of Guernsey, I believe. The other one sports the French tri-couleur, and you can almost smell the garlic from its galley."

Myriam called back: "I do smell the garlic. But what I'd prefer would be to taste wine from its cave."

David and Aida also relished the fact that their jobs at the tiller had almost come to an end. But there was the worry about their general appearance. "By Jove, but my hair's a mess," Aida complained.

"What about me: still in my swimming trunks! Take the tiller one last time, Aida, while I go into the cabin and put on a dry T-shirt and jeans."

Aida chose to follow the Guernsey sailboat to its dock. She preferred to use a British boat. She knew there could be legal complications for having entered the London area of the Thames without informing the Harbour Master

Dennis, although busily coughing now from the onset of his heavy cold, knew in his gut how important it was for him to stay within the law. He felt determined not to end in a London prison due to this untoward, sad experience. Could he be suspected of killing Herb? Would British police arrest him when they examined the hematoma on Herb's forehead, thinking it had been done deliberately? Should he be prepared for an insinuation that he'd pushed Herb into the water?

While still at the tiller, Dennis was stopped by the boat of a maritime dock guard, who shouted it wasn't admissible to enter the marina area of St. Katherine Docks without having telephoned, radioed, or written to their dockmaster.

He put on an act as if he was a curious tourist who hadn't a care in the world.

With a fake grin, he left Aida in charge of the vessel, and Myriam continuing her vigil of Herb's body.

Dennis jumped on to dry land and quickly located a public telephone to advise Uncle of Herb's accidental death, and the fact that Herb's body was on board his investor friend's sailboat.

Uncle agreed immediately with the plan for him to claim Herb's body and turn it over to a Muslim mortician. Dennis also brought up the subject of advising his investor that the yacht and Jaguar car would not be returned by his guests. The yacht would need to be collected and taken to the East Brighton Sailing Club, once Herb's body was removed. "Perhaps the Muslim mortician would provide paperwork for the Jaguar's rental company," Dennis added carefully, not treading overly on Uncle's grief yet passing on information that could avoid him jailtime, "Verifying that the lessor was dead and the car still in the East Brighton Sailing Club's car park. Oh, Uncle, I'm so deeply sorry that—"

Uncle put aside all gentlemanly pretense to interrupt. Through manly sobs, he managed: "All expenses will be paid. Everything taken care of. I will be on the dock as soon as I've found a proper mortician."

His voice came through the receiver, broken, but showing he was determined to make all the funeral arrangements according to Sharia Law.

Within a quarter of an hour he joined Dennis on the pier, showed credentials, and had a substitute dockmaster speak by telephone with the sailboat's investor-owner.

No time was lost to have Herb's body transferred into the Muslim mortician's van, that had arrived simultaneously with Uncle and the Iman from Aida's mosque.

Both women left the sailboat, Myriam carrying the two swimsuits while Aida clutched her sweater that sagged as if it had been in a monsoon.

Aida excused herself to rush to call Coutts Bank to explain why she had missed work, and needed extra time to attend a funeral.

Wiping the unending tears that still coursed down both cheeks like mountain streams, Myriam asked: "What time will the funeral take place? Do we have time to go to our cottage and change into more appropriate clothes?"

Solemnly, but with considerable compassion, the Iman suggested that Dennis tell Uncle the precise time of Herb's death.

"We finished lunch at the club about one p.m., then had about half an hour's pleasant sailing, while a storm engulfed us. Then Herb raced for another twenty-four hours. Herb handed the tiller to me several times, mainly to visit the head, but it was twilight when he went to check the jib. He'd only gone a few yards when a blast of wind caught the boat in such a way that the boom came about. Herb didn't notice until too late. He was knocked into the water. I'd say somewhere around six o'clock, yesterday."

Uncle, in abysmal despair, struggled to recoup his aura of distinguished gentleman. "My dears, the Rolls is outside. Have you had anything to eat? Coffee? I'll keep you company until the Rolls takes you to your homes. May I add, I'm truly mortified that you have gone through this experience, but I have to thank you for bringing me Halo's body. I intend to join in the cleansing and shrouding ceremonies myself."

In the Rolls Royce, nobody talked. The ride for Dennis was like being back in church as a little boy. But before they arrived at Claridge's, Dennis made a point of repeating some of Herb's last words to Uncle. He deleted the part about guessing Uncle's plan, but accentuated Herb's intention to do Hajj next year. "Herb's last thought was to please Allah."

Those words brought a measure of comfort, but were displaced by Uncle groaning: "How can I ever explain to his parents my part in this horror?"

Dennis, who was getting a very sore throat and blocked sinuses, wanted to say: Don't try! Tell them that I said Herb had a good time at Ascot and racing the yacht off East Brighton. But instead, Dennis permitted the heavy silence to return.

On the drive to Epping, a new, racking cough added its misery.

After arriving home, Dennis hoped that a hot bath would ease his symptoms. It didn't help.

Earlier, at Claridge's, Myriam had given her heartfelt sympathy to Uncle.

At home, she brewed hot chocolate for Dennis, but that didn't help.

Dressing for the funeral, Dennis coughed out: "I don't own a sweater. I've looked right through my old duffle bag: no sweater."

"Your business suit came with a vest. Use that. You sound like you're coming down with a cold."

"Yes. But I'm not going to miss Herb's funeral. Do you have the phone number for a taxi? Forget going by bus. It's raining hard, and the wind has followed us all the way here."

"Uncle's car is outside. He's waving from the window. Come on, darling. I was fond of Herb in my own way. And I believe you were too."

The incessant rain and unobliging wind tossed the five thousand pound Rolls Royce as if it was a toy.

Nobody had an umbrella, including Uncle's hired chauffeur. All three were drenched. Their clothes soaked, their shoes saturated with mud.

Separated, Myriam climbed upstairs to where women were allowed to pray.

On the main floor, Uncle and Dennis found the ceremony already in progress. Herb's naked body lay spread out for the cleansing. Several paid mourners were washing him. Uncle rushed to join them, feeling deeply sorry that he'd arrived late.

Myriam found Aida already in the women's upstairs section. Aida was blanketed in prayers. She barely acknowledged Myriam.

Feeling very uncomfortable, Myriam wanted this grim aftermath to end.

But she tried to reach the Aida she thought she knew. She whispered: "I'm glad we aren't permitted to be in with Herb's naked body. I don't think I could take that."

Aida said nothing. Her lips were still moving in silent prayer. Myriam recognized that Aida was hiding her emotions. When so often Aida had declared how much she loved her work at Coutts, had she really been dreaming of moving to Brooklyn to make a cozy home there with Herb as her husband? Could it be that she'd fallen in love with bad-mouthed Herb, in spite of his put-off manner? Would she ever admit her dreams to Dennis, at Coutts? Aida had made it obvious that she was distancing herself from happily married Myriam, ensconced with Dennis in their cozy home in Epping.

Dennis, already familiar with the proceedings from the washing and shrouding event aboard the DEVERON, spent the entire ceremony attempting to control his coughing.

The shrouding was accelerated because the twenty-four hour deadline was approaching quickly. The Iman discouraged Uncle from accompanying Herb's remains to the burial grounds. "Our mortuary man has ambulance privileges. His vehicle uses flashing lights and beeping horns to move through traffic and red lights. You would arrive twenty minutes later, when the coffin was already in its grave."

There was no wake. Following what Dennis would describe as "the service," Uncle disappeared into Claridge's Hotel to go directly to his suite to mourn alone. Again, no conversation had taken place in the car.

Dennis and Myriam did hear from Uncle on the following day. He telephoned them to say he'd learned that the DEVERON was journeying to Alexandria, sailing that evening, and he had arranged at Coutts for Dennis to leave work early to accompany him to Southampton to say "goodbye" on the DEVERON.

Out of consideration for what he always termed "Myriam's delicate condition," Uncle hadn't invited Myriam to accompany him to the ship.

"Nobody's going to stop me from going to see Captain Igleton and the deveron," Myriam stated flatly. "I'll take a bus to Coutts and you can expect me there at the main door to meet you in Coutts front door."

The rain had eased and the wind had dispersed, but Dennis had not got rid of his cold. His coughs were more resonant, and his eyeballs' veins were like the red feathers on the wings of a cardinal.

Uncle had shrunk. Doubled up in the back seat, with what looked like an onset of osteoporosis, he stared at Dennis and Myriam as if they were strangers on a train.

It was Captain Igleton who brought cheer. Enchanted at the sight of Myriam, now so much a settled London housewife, he brought laughter and hope to those two who were still mourning Herb. He told how another young lady had stowed away on his ship that day, hoping to marry his love-struck Purser. "But this time she was escorted off the ship. She is one young lady who must wait for the DEVERON'S next trip to London to hear wedding bells. No Bermuda certificate for her!"

When the warning gongs sounded, Uncle made an effort once again to be the complete gentleman. Uncle thanked Myriam and Dennis for the friendship they'd offered Herb during his last days on earth. He acknowledged that Dennis had done his best to carry out his original plan. With a sad small gesture for goodbye, Uncle disappeared below deck.

No paper streamers or confetti were thrown at DEVERON's sparse group of passengers.

Dennis stood stoically recalling past times with a friendly nod to former work mates dealing with lines from the dock. He'd moved on without forgetting his experiences on the DEVERON, but one of his ex-bunks mates shook him from complacency.

"Dennis!" Ahmed yelled into the combative wind.

"Over to your right. Watch me..." From the DEVERON's mushy lower deck, Ahmed took a death-defying leap to arrive at Dennis's side on the dock. "Old friend.. So much news to tell..." Dennis grabbed into air attempting to keep Ahmed from falling between the crushing side of DEVERON and the concrete dock.

Ahmed managed that starring role on his own. With one damp leg, Ahmed made landfall on a protruding spar.

Dennis bellowed: "What do you think you're doing? Ahmed, you could have been killed! And how can you afford to jump ship?"

"Not jumping ship. Know how to meet the DEVERON with a harbor pilot. Harbor's congested. I'll make it back aboard all right. Dennis, there is so much news…"

"Ahmed, tell me quickly. And let's exchange shoes: yours are ruined."

"Your feet are bigger than mine. Also, you sound like you have a bad cold! Need dry shoes. Dennis, have you heard I married Ili?"

"But, Ili's married to Mehmet."

Grinning widely through his shivers, Ahmed gloated:

"Not anymore! A tattletale found out that Mehmet had used a forger for a faked deed, so that he could get Ili into the bedroom of that apartment. He had only paid the first installment on a mortgage. And he had been selling his friends for money."

"I finally learned he was on the take at the Al Hasa Oasis. I saw Mehmet pushing banknotes into a very sizeable briefcase. He'd given my whereabouts to one of the thugs who scouted for Myriam's father."

"Ili's parents felt so ashamed that she was married to such a liar. A traitor! They were quite pleased to allow her to marry me after I got my divorce from Fila."

"Didn't they demand you give her the deed for an apartment?"

"No problem. Remember I have owned an apartment in Cairo. Poor Ili 's worth in the marriage market had tumbled in devout Alexandria. Even her grandparents were glad she had a prospective husband in me. Yes, and I was being paid more money, too. I have been promoted from shoveling coal. I am a waiter, now!"

"Welcome to the ranks of the clean."

"There is more."

"Tell, but be quick. This wind is freezing."

"You should take something for your flu. Remember when we were both terrified we might catch tuberculosis from Seth? Speaking of diseases: Fila has married

Mehmet. No other woman would have him, and do not forget she has that disease I had caught in Barcelona…"

"What about Ili? Have you given it to her?"

"No. I went to doctors until I was cured before our wedding. Ili is pregnant, our marriage has been blessed by Allah."

"My marriage has been a happy one too. Myriam is in her fourth month. But, Fila… She—"

"I believe you Americans say: 'You Can't Teach An Old Dog New Tricks…' She's a lost woman. But Dennis, let us speak of happier days. You have new clothes. Did you find a job? An apartment?"

"Yes. Good job. Little cottage. We're staying in England. I don't want to go to U.S.A. where I'm branded a Sexual Offender. Ahmed, there's the pilot boat you need. Wave it over. I'll look for you next time DEVERON comes into port. Thanks for the news. Best luck to Ili."

Ahmed gave another mighty jump. This time he landed squarely on the rain-washed pilot boat's narrow planks.

With a wave, Ahmed merged into advancing fog.

Still battling Southampton's unwelcoming wind, Myriam had kept waving adoringly at busy Captain Igleton until DEVERON's frothing wake he went.

Chapter 14

Southampton, England

There was no Rolls Royce to transport Myriam and Dennis back to London. Uncle's leased Rolls Royce had started its term with him in Southampton, and to Southampton it had been returned.

Myriam and Dennis took the Southampton-to-London express.

They had a compartment to themselves. Myriam used the privacy to broach a delicate bit of news: "Mommy will be arriving here next week."

"No! Your father will have those Saudi thugs find you, by following her. Anyway, our baby's room won't hold an adult. Too small."

"Mommy won't be staying with us because she rented a house in Epping, she's bringing her sick sister with her. And, my darling dearest one, there will never again be Saudi thugs sent by my father to find me. He had a massive stroke. Can't move. Can't speak. Can't think. A Trustee has been appointed to run his companies. He's permanently hospitalized."

"Sweetheart, how do you know all these things?"

"News came in this morning's mail."

"Could be fake. A trap to make you let down your guard."

"No, darling. Hand-written by Mommy. On her engraved letterhead paper. All we have to worry about is that you might give your cold to Mommy. Or, to me. But I, for one, won't mind it if you do."

Myriam leaned closer, pushing to bring together their two bodies. She raised her mouth for their special McLeary-invented kiss.

The train's whistle wasn't loud enough to drown out the sound of their special, luscious kisses.

Rapture.

Biography of
Beatrice Fairbanks Cayzer

Beatrice Fairbanks Cayzer D.St.L is the daughter of a former U.S. Ambassador-at-Large, most notable as a Negotiator who ended the Peruvian-Ecuadorian War, and for his portfolio for Secretary of War Woodring on keeping Puerto Rico in the U.S. Commonwealth in order to maintain its strategic position as a defense for the Panama Canal. She was educated at Marymount School, Oakwood Friends Academy, and Barnard College. After living for a time with her God-Mother First Lady of Ecuador Elena de Arroyo del Rio, she married President Arroyo's nephew Alfredo Holguin, son of the Colombian Ambassador to Ecuador. They had three daughters, Mary, Eugenie, and Claudia. Her second marriage was to Major H. Stanley Cayzer, a Second World War hero (North African Campaign) much admired later as an environmentalist for his measures to save Scottish grouse from extinction. His uncle, Admiral Lord Jellicoe was First Sea Lord and later became Governor of New Zealand. For ten years she lived between Eaton Square London, the Scottish Sporting Estate in Aberdeenshire, Westcote Manor in Warwickshir, until they moved to Guernsey, during which time she was named Woman of the Year. She became a British Citizen while residing in the Channel Islands. Their next move was to Monaco, where they shared their away time between London and Palm Beach, Florida. She wrote over one thousand travel and society articles, her published books include TALES OF PALM BEACH, THE PRINCES AND THE PRINCESSES

OF WALES, The Royal World of Animals, Drugstore, DIANE, Love Love in Darfur, The Secret Diary of Mrs. John Quincy Adams, (eleven times on the Best Seller List) and ten Happy Harrow mysteries including Murder by Medicine, and the Happy Harrow Murder Trilogy (twenty times on the Best Seller List). Her latest novel is How to Save a Child (three times on the Best Seller List). In 2016, she married Environmentalist William Richards II. As a racehorse owner she won at Doncaster (where her sister in law had won a classic, The St. Leger). For her racing partner Beatrice was fortunate to share horses with Sir James Scott, Lord Lieutenant of Hampshire. In her background she counts as a direct ancestor Henry Adams, who settled in Massachusetts in 1634, progenitor of President John Adams, President John Quincy Adams, and Vice President Charles Warren Fairbanks (in first Administration of Theodore Roosevelt.)

Her European clubs include Cavalry & Guards (London), Channel Islands Yacht Club (Guernsey), Yacht Club de Monaco, Race Horse Owners (England)and the Jockey Club Rooms of Newmarket. In Palm Beach her clubs are Bath & Tennis, English Speaking Union, The Society of the Four Acts, the Preservation Society, the DAR, the CDA, and the Descendants of the Mayflower Society.